T0316530

The Switch

Mary Karooro Okurut

FEMRITE - Uganda Women Writers Association
P.O. Box 705, Kampala.
Tel: +256 414 543943 / +256 772 743943
Email: info@femriteug.org
www.femriteug.org

First Published 2016

ISBNISBN:978-9970-480-08-1

Book Design: Ronald Ssali

Printed by: FEAM Investments ltd

The Switch

Mary Karooro Okurut

FEMRITE PUBLICATIONS LIMITED

Foreword

Every time I start reading any of Hon. Karooro's books, I do not put it down until I come to the end. The first one I read was, *The Official Wife.* I was traveling from Kampala to Moroto in North Eastern Uganda. I usually like to marvel at the beautiful scenery of the Pearl of Africa, but this time, through the 466 Kilometer journey, I was completely engulfed in reading the book. This is the experience I have every time I read her books. *The Switch*, is no exception.

The book you are about to read does not only show the depth of the physical and emotional trauma that female genital mutilation brings to women and girls, but also health consequences that they can experience through their life time.

When Hon. Karooro told me of her desire to write a book on female genital mutilation, she was then the Minister of Gender, Labour and Social Development. I spent the whole evening reflecting on this, for I had read some of her books and I was impressed by her style – she strongly brings out issues affecting women with such powerful imagery. I knew that with her sharp humour, she would justly handle the delicate cultural ritual of female genital mutilation. She doesn't let me down.

Through the flashbacks of a young woman, Tezira Chelimo, the reader feels her fear as she struggles to keep her dark secret from a man she loves so dearly.

Chelimo went through the ritual of female genital mutilation to fulfill the cultural requirement as a rite of passage from childhood to womanhood and eligibility for marriage.

When she regains the courage to tell her secret so she can say 'yes' to her lover's proposal for marriage, unspeakable challenges await her in marriage. The switch had been turned off!

Female Genital Mutilation is by far one of the worst forms of injustice and a human rights violation that a woman or a girl can ever experience. Besides the physical pain, it is a big threat to a woman's or a girl's reproductive health. When a woman or a girl is cut, it can cause prolonged bleeding. Sometimes, the cutting can become infectious, and in the long-run can spark off a whole range of gynecological problems, including fistula and complications during child birth.

This book is a big step towards addressing Female Genital Mutilation. Just like her other literature, Hon. Karooro is so courageous in her choice of words. She powerfully gives a comprehensive description of the ritual, the reasons why it is practiced, the social cultural and economic dynamics, as well as the effects.

As the story unfolds, you will see the role that the community and government can play to address this culturally deep rooted practice that hurts women and girls. The Author's poetic style gives the reader interest to search deeper into how the communities can give up the practice without giving up the positive aspects of culture. Through *The Switch*, it is clear that story-telling is a powerful tool that can be used to mobilize citizens against any forms of injustice.

On behalf of UNFPA, the United Nations Population Fund, I am truly privileged to be associated with such great work of literature on a topic that touches the core of the Fund's mandate. *The Switch* illuminates the sense of womanhood and the quest of every Sabiny, Pokot, or Tepeth young girl to become one without having to go through the painful ritual of female genital mutilation.

Esperance Fundira
Country Representative
United Nations Population Fund (UNFPA)

Acknowledgement

I appreciate the major role of UNFPA in supporting this book right from the inception of the idea to the point of publication.

I am grateful to one of the strongest activists against Female Genital Mutilation, Ms Beatrice Chelangat; for it was she who tickled my mind just fine as I sought the appropriate title for this novel.

I also wish to thank Mr. Benjamin Sabila of *The New Vision* who spearheaded the background research on the ground in Kapchorwa District. Without his extraordinary diligence, this book would not be.

My sincere gratitude further goes to my editors, Hilda Twongyeirwe and Gawaya Tegulle who spent long hours at their computers doing quality checks;

And my two beloved – and lovely – girls Joan and Maureen who kept on censoring the language as I wrote; all the while screaming "Mummy, don't be too candid!". I hearkened to their voice.

To my readers, I feel honoured, because you keep me writing.

To you all I say, *Keyitabon koromun* - thank you very much!

Chapter One

With the construction boom in recent years, the sight of construction cranes looming on the horizon had become ubiquitous all over the Kampala City Skyline. Analysts predicted that the same sight would, in the near future, meet the eye in other big towns across Uganda, if the economy kept growing as fast.

The introduction of large foreign traders into the country – mostly from China, India and other parts of Western Europe – had excited many industrialists, particularly in the real estate sector, where builders and developers hoped to benefit from an increased demand for retail spaces. The increased rural-urban migration, which in Uganda's case usually meant people moving from the villages to the capital city, also meant that a city originally built to house half a million, now had six times that number.

So as the spaces got fewer in the Central Business District, CBD, the keen eyes of Real Estate developers began scanning the suburbs, starting with the better-known ones in the immediate vicinity of the CBD-Kamwokya, Muyenga, Bukoto, Naguru and the like – that were deemed fashionable to occupy. But soon even those quickly began to experience congestion, and the real estate scavengers began to scramble for Ntinda.

Analysts started to predict a marked increase in demand for commercial real estate, warehousing and office space; but also for quality residential real estate, targeting the young corporates who wanted housing not too far from the CBD, and where the roads were fairly decent and where they'd have no need to brave mud and dust daily, to get home. As the number of developments went up, the rates came down, enabling more and more people to access quality residences without too much trouble.

Quickly and quietly, the population in Ntinda exploded; more people came from all over the country and from abroad. The houses available in central Ntinda were quickly gobbled up and the expansion outside Ntinda began to take shape. But those with more money saw that there was still room in Ntinda – as long as one built upwards, rather than horizontally. You could potentially build up to the moon if the conditions were right and you would not be breaking any law. Only your money would limit you. And within a short time, the bigger-moneyed folks began buying out those with old bungalows, and quickly started building high rise buildings that gave one a good view of the entire surrounding.

One such building was Parade House; a seven floor affair in Ministers' village, one of the more upscale neighbourhoods of the satellite town. Folks were too busy to inquire into the security implications of such a high rise building in an area where the high and mighty resided. They were more focused on finding out who had built it and where the money had come from. That is why nobody deemed it necessary to ask any questions when a new tenant moved into Flat 7 of Parade House.

But again to be fair, this was not the village where everybody knew everybody else. This was town;

and in town you simply shared the roads and the air you breathed. And you also had the same president and the same God, nothing else. Nobody cared to know who their neighbour was or what they did for a living. You came and went as you pleased, minded your own business and you were glad when everybody else did mind their own business too.

So when Simon Adeni moved into Flat 7, nobody paid any attention. And they had no real cause for concern, because Adeni – a man who had very few words in his vocabulary besides 'no', 'shut up' or some other disagreeable grunt, was a man whose military training had taught the value of being able to be in a place without being noticed. He was able to melt into a crowd as easily as fish slipped into water – smooth, calm and swift.

Flat 7 was not very popular with tenants for the reason that it was on the seventh floor of a building that had no lifts. Folks were reluctant to have to go up and down such a long flight of stairs all the time, especially if they had families, or returned home each evening with arms heavily laden with all kinds of groceries and other home necessities.

So when Adeni came looking for a suitable house to rent, Flat 7 had never had tenants ever since Parade House was constructed a year before. With the building boom around the city and indeed the country, rental space was no longer hard to come by, as had been the case in previous decades. There was lots of rental space in the city centre, and at very affordable rates.

Outside the city centre there was even more rental space that came cheaper.

Adeni spent the next few days assembling his team and equipment. No one paid attention to the quiet fellow. He liked to mind his own business. He was the perfect neighbour.

*****

On the seventh floor of the building, the workmen installed several cameras at various angles. By the end of the day, Arthur, the young man at the control room – a large affair fitted with several video screens, reported that he could monitor all activities in the minister's compound, as long as it took place on the eastern side of the house. He added that a few more cameras from the other side of the house would help complete the picture.

"We shall handle that in due course," said Adeni. "Your task will be to ensure that the timers are all perfect and that we can know with precision what took place at what time."

"No problem," said Arthur as he opened a box of cereal and poured some of it into a bowl of warm milk. He added two spoonfuls of sugar and stirred..

"We'll be able to do anything you like boss." He scooped some of the cereal into his mouth, tasted it around his tongue and liking the taste, he sat down to enjoy it.

*****

Adeni was never in a hurry. For two months, he and his boys kept tabs on the minister's residence and the movement of both minister and daughter. Three cameras – all of them motion sensitive – were directed on the minister's residence, covering the gate, compound and the more visible part of the house. A fourth camera was roving, just to pick up every other movement that could not possibly be picked up by the three fixed cameras. On a motorbike – never the same bike or clothes twice in the same week – Adeni followed the minister's car to her office.

Every evening Arthur, after sifting through all the footage, briefed Adeni on what he had seen, what trends he had identified and whatever patterns he had established. Arthur had been chosen because not only was he a wizard with electronics, especially computers, cameras and cell phones, he was also meticulous with detail. And he had a rare ability to analyze data and draw appropriate and brilliant conclusions.

Adeni listened carefully to Arthur's analysis every evening, made notes continuously and only paused to ask questions. Over time he had come to trust Arthur's judgment. The boy seldom put a foot wrong.

After two months, Arthur was able to conclude that the minister was a very organized person.

"Which is a mistake," observed Adeni thoughtfully, more to himself than anybody else. "No security-conscious person should ever establish a schedule, because they give their adversaries an advantage."

"The Minister leaves for her office by six every weekday morning with the young girl. She drops her at Lohana High School, and then proceeds to her office. The girl is usually brought back by the driver. It is only on one occasion that we have observed the Minister returning her daughter from school." said Arthur.

"So when does the driver pick the girl?"

"After four o'clock, as she is in Senior Two. Apparently the mother doesn't want her to stay behind for other activities."

"What time do they arrive home?"

"Four-thirty."

By the end of the fortnight that followed, Adeni was able to predict whatever was going to happen in the ministerial household, a task made very easy by the fact that the minister was a stickler to schedule.

"Very stupid," he said, after observing the footage over and over. "Very stupid."

Adeni scrutinised all possible ways of how to get the girl, patiently turning each option upside down. He dug deeper into the situation, wondering about the possibility of any window of opportunity. The girl was never out of sight of an adult supervisor. But he knew that there was always at least one such likelihood in every security arrangement: a lapse of concentration, a gap that might not have been identified, a minimal leeway that could be exploited. "There will surely be a window," he mused aloud.

It was well into the tenth week of patient exploration and study of footage when Arthur made an observation that made Adeni's heart sing.

"The guards are only extremely alert when the minister is approaching," he pointed out. "They even never seem to bother opening the gate when the driver returns the young girl home. The small entrance at the gate is always open in the evenings. When the driver and the girl arrive home every evening, the driver opens the small gate. Most of the time the guards are dozing when the girl returns home. It might be because they are awake the entire night and so they try to catch sleep before dusk and before the Minister returns home," reported Arthur. He clicked the next footage in play and showed the driver stopping. The driver left the engine running, entered through the small entrance and proceeded to unlock the gate from inside. He took his time. He then jumped back into the car and eased it through the gate. Adeni watched seven different versions of footage and each told the same story with minimal, if any, alterations.

That was where the weakness was: the minister's penchant for being particular. That was going to be her undoing. They had established too predictable a pattern. Adeni wondered who was in charge of the minister's security arrangements. The most basic rule for personal security is; do not follow patterns because patterns are dangerous. Habits must be ruled out completely, as a keen enemy eye could easily predict what each next move would be and then strike, with disastrous effects. Any person in charge of security should know this basic rule.

There was another big lapse: the guards were, in their own psyche, deployed to protect the minister. Not much thought had been given to her family members. They slept during the day. Maybe they presumed that murderers or robbers did their work at night.

Adeni went back to the important discovery he had made.

"This is where our big break will be," he told Fabio later that evening. "The fact that the driver leaves his key in the ignition and the engine stays running means we have exactly 60 seconds to get the girl.

"Whatever we do must be timed to last 40 seconds. The 20 extra seconds will only come in handy when we have a last minute unforeseen turn of events and we need to get away. But that would be disaster because if we fail then, she is gone for good. Nobody ever gave much thought to the fact that somebody may want to kidnap a minister's daughter. It only happens in the movies and Uganda is oceans away from Hollywood. For the next two weeks before the minister's Kapchorwa programme, we must do our rehearsals over and over, until we are sure nothing can thwart our intent."

Fabio nodded his assent; took a long pull at the cigarette in his mouth and casually blew a steady stream of smoke into the air above him. He was thinking, his forehead creasing into folds.

Fabio had small eyes that moved soft but swift in their sockets, taking and soaking in everything around him, especially when it was dark. His mouth was small. His friends always said that was the reason he always ate very little. But he always explained to them that his eating habits had been influenced by the many years in military training. And the little mouth brought out even less than it took in, because Fabio said little or nothing most of the time. The only exception to this general rule was that he liked to spit a lot; owing in part to the fact that his pipe and cigarette were never far from him. So he spat out of habit. But he also spat even more whenever he was on tension. It was for him, the equivalent of throwing a tantrum. Whenever he was in deep thought, his mouth hung half-open and his tongue darted around in his mouth, something that gave him the look of a busy little snake on the prowl.

What few people knew was that Fabio was actually a snake and more. He was as good with a gun as he was with man to man combat. Because of his small size, almost every one of his enemies made the fatal mistake of underestimating him and they all paid a high price. Fabio was quick with his hands and even faster with his feet, and packed a good punch. He could throw a knife with exactitude and was not afraid to spill people's blood, brains and intestines. His enemies often died a miserable death.

When he quit the army, where he had distinguished himself on the frontline as a precision shooter and ruthless killer, Fabio had retired to Bwaise, a busy slummy suburb north of Kampala city, where nobody knew about him or his past. Only a few of his colleagues from the army days knew about him and maintained contact with him for whenever there was any dirty work to be done. Adeni was one of those that knew how useful Fabio was. He was indispensable to Adeni.

"Just one small problem," Fabio began slowly, puffing away. Adeni looked up.

"If the Minister will be in Kapchorwa on the third of December, then chances are that she will have gone with the driver. Whoever brings back the child in the afternoon may behave differently. Where would that leave our nice little plan?"

Adeni smiled and continued. "As a matter of procedure," he explained patiently, "Lohana High School does not allow strangers to pick up kids. If Samson picks the kid every day, it is unlikely anybody else will be designated to carry out that delicate task. Only two or three people can ordinarily be allowed to pick her up other than her mother or that driver. These would have to be familiar persons that the child knows and with authentic authorisation."

"And then two very very important points," observed Fabio. "One, where do we keep the girl after the capture? Two, how do we transport her to Kapchorwa?"

There was a minute of heavy silence as Adeni stroked his goatee. Then slowly, he began to speak.

"To the first question; we take the girl in a place they'd be less likely to suspect."

"And pray, where would this hiding place be?" Fabio inquired.

"Right in the minister's own backyard."

"Meaning?"

"Meaning in the first few hours or minutes, we keep her next door. Nobody would think of searching in the Minister's neighbourhood. And when security is relaxed, we take her in broad daylight, to a place that no one can suspect."

"You will tell us which place. But, why would we do it in broad daylight?"

"Simply because nobody would suspect us to move her during day time."

Fabio nodded his head in affirmation.

"And the transport? Do we hire a car or trek on foot for half a year to Kapchorwa?"

Adeni laughed for just a few seconds before his lips resumed their normal calm pose. "Very funny. None of the above," he said. "We use an ambulance."

"And where would we get an ambulance from?"

"Just borrow one." Adeni never stole. He always 'borrowed.'

"That would be too much work, it would cause unnecessary trouble. It is easy to trace a stolen ambulance. This is a very small country. I don't like the sound of it," said Fabio.

"Then we use one of the black hearses from one of the funeral services."

"What is a hearse?"

"Really Fabio! You must have been the least intelligent student in your class!"

Fabio's brow creased in dangerous annoyance as he got up threateningly.

"Sorry chap. No offence meant. A hearse is that black van or car that transports dead bodies. We must assume that the security people will be looking for a live person and they won't start by checking among the dead. I have a telephone number of a colleague from one of the funeral homes. That chap owes me a favour."

Adeni started dialling on his mobile phone. He set the phone in his palm and he pressed the loudspeaker button.

"Hello Adeni. What makes you…"

"Hi Phillip. Look, I need something from you very urgently."

Phillip's laughter cracked through the telephone.

"All your needs are always of utmost urgency. But there is no problem as long as you can wait till tomorrow," Phillip said.

"Phillip, this can't wait," Adeni swore under his breath-but it was loud enough for Phillip to hear and know that something was afoot. Phillip sighed.

"Okay roll," he said

"I need to borrow a hearse," said Adeni

"It is safe to assume from your tone that nobody has died, right?"

"Right."

"And nobody is going to die."

"Nobody."

"And this conversation never took place."

"Never."

"Then we have a deal. I'll be ready whenever you are."

"Thanks buddy," Adeni said as a rugged, chubby finger touched the 'off' button on the phone. Both men smiled with satisfaction.

"Of course you know Fabio, that a hearse has the right of way. No police officer or any law enforcement officer stops a hearse. No stopping at roadblocks too. No inconvenience. Nothing. No observance of traffic lights. The hearse usually has two or three other cars in their procession; the vehicle carrying the spouse and or children, another with close family members and sometimes another with friends, well-wishers, enemies and everybody else. All of them are almost always allowed to break all the traffic rules."

The two men chuckled and hit a high-five.

*****

Nobody said anything when a few young men clad in yellow and blue tracksuits and wearing bright red helmets and going about on roller skates, began moving around the neighborhood. It was assumed that the smoother roads in Ministers' Village made for much better skating than the rough, uneven variety in the other areas. Because they came every morning before the sun came out and every evening as the sun prepared to go to bed, nobody even thought twice about them. They were just some young people having a good time.

And as they didn't look armed, or even interested in the plush residences that graced the street, even the guards in various homes didn't pay attention to them. Neither did the young men pay attention to the guards. They simply enjoyed parading themselves in the yellow and blue tracksuits and they were especially delighted with the goggles that came with the outfit. And they were contented with the twenty thousand shillings they received from Adeni everyday for just skating around Ministers' Village. And they were eternally grateful that Adeni had indicated they could keep the roller skates and uniforms after their two week assignment was over. They would not be seen again anywhere near Ministers Village from the third of December. And none of them came from anywhere nearby. They were each selected from the lowest echelons of society and would have no need to be anywhere in this neighbourhood in the foreseeable future – it was almost certain they'd never be seen again in this neighbourhood.

Nobody cared about the fact that they seemed to be on Martyrs Drive Road at exactly the same time in the morning and in the evening. Adeni had thought about the risk this posed, especially if some security-conscious chap captured the pattern, but figured he could take his chances.

The skaters were all over the road every morning when the Minister and her daughter left in the morning, and they always never cared who was in the car in the first place and they wouldn't have cared less even if they had known at all. But more importantly, Adeni had made sure none of them knew who he was or why he wanted them to skate. He had talked vaguely of a skating competition that was coming soon, and how he was building a good team of young skaters. They'd do their practice runs in Ministers' village for a fortnight, then shift to Makindye Division for another fortnight, after which their readiness for the big time would be assessed. The fact that they had another pair of skates and a different set of uniforms was incentive enough for the young men, even without the daily allowance. But Adeni knew only too well the importance of strong incentives when you had a do or die task at hand.

When the skaters got going, Adeni was happy to note that nobody took more than a passing glance at the young men. They were just little fellows having a good time. They'd have a rest day after the morning performance of December 3rd, after which they'd resume their runs in Makindye; he assured them every evening when they met at the Kyambogo Primary School playground. As it was always dark by the time they got to Kyambogo, Adeni was sure none of the boys could recognize him if they saw him again.

The only person who took interest in the skaters was the Minister's driver Samson, who had to wait for them to pass before he could get the car on the road. In the evening when he returned the little girl home, he only had to be sure he didn't run over any of them. After a while they became part of the scenery and he no longer considered them an issue.

From the seventh floor, Arthur captured every moment in and around the Minister's compound on his screens once in a while, by casually glancing at the window, as he dug through a bowel of cornflakes or some other cereal.

*****

Adeni was tense in the days leading to third December. He had gone through such tension many times before, such as in the army days – the butterflies in the tummy that preceded an important mission. He felt the same sensation every time Manchester United was playing a big side in an important game. He had grown used to it. But the enormity of this mission did more than tickle the butterflies in his stomach. He discovered he had to make use of the toilet more times than usual, as the contemplation of both success and failure hit him hard.

The morning of third December began precisely in the way he did not want it to begin. The heavens opened and pounded the earth with a vengeance at dawn. Sheets of rain and gusts of wind tore through the atmosphere and onto the earth's surface. Fortunately, by six in the morning, the rain had eased to a steady stream of droplets. Even the skaters were able to do their run, meeting the minister's vehicle as she left the house.

Adeni followed the minister's car at a distance, to confirm that they'd dropped the girl at Lohana. The minister proceeded to her office perhaps to handle a few formalities. A few minutes later she emerged out of her office and she was enroute to Kapchorwa. Adeni observed with satisfaction that Samson did not leave with the minister. Adeni went back to the base and began working out the final details of his plan.

*****

Adeni sent out surveillance teams. On the stroke of four o'clock, Samson pulled into the parking lot of Lohana High School. He seemed more relaxed than usual, perhaps because the boss was away and she would not be back for another three or so days. This was time for Samson to devote a little more time to his wife who perhaps saw very little of him with the minister's presence.

Samson's gaze was on the horizon as the Minister's daughter got into the car. He was silent as he drove along Prince Charles Drive, through Lugogo By-Pass and into Kira Road. He grunted vague replies to the girl's incessant chatter, and pressed the buttons on the car radio. Most drivers were into the habit of listening to music all the time even during the News Hour or other important talk shows. It was probable that Samson was listening to music instead of news briefs on Capital FM.

Adeni's research had established that Samson was building. He too must have been affected by the rising cost of construction materials. Everybody was building these days, and the chaps with hardware shops were making a daily killing. It was easy to build when one had a job like that of a driver. One could always ask for a salary advance and then live on field and safari allowances that came with being a minister's driver. Bank loans with crazy interest rates were out of the question.

*****

The familiar sight of chaps in yellow and blue tracksuits did not interrupt Samson, as over the past fortnight he'd come to expect to meet them morning and evening.

He did not notice that they were much fewer this time. Just two of them. Neither did he pay attention to the fact that they were slightly bigger and much older. This time they had goggles and helmets on.

He did not pay attention to the two skaters who were taking their time, skating casually behind him. Neither did he look back when he disembarked from the car, leaving the engine running as usual, to go inside the compound and open the gate.

As soon as Samson disappeared through the small gate, the smaller of the two skaters jumped onto the driver's seat. His colleague jumped in beside him and sat next to the girl. His hand quickly covered her mouth to keep her from making any noise. Samson was just beginning to slide back the bolt of the gate, when Fabio drove off. By the time he emerged out of the gate, he was just in time to see the car disappearing round the corner. He made a loud alarm, frantically calling to the guards who were sleeping in the guard house. He ran down the road trying to chase after a car he very well knew he could never catch up with. There was nobody else on the road within eye-distance which was always the issue with Ministers' Village. Most people in this village were old men and women who were no longer in the productive age bracket. As such, they came home at their leisure. The minister's car was gone. But more alarming, her only child was gone too. Samson collapsed onto the tarmac and bawled like a baby.

From the Seventh Floor of Parade Building, Arthur had paused in his cereal-eating spree to catch the action live. The arrival of the car had left the cereal-laden spoon mid-air. It had stayed there all through the action. It was not until the car disappeared into the distance that the cereal finally reached its destination.

"Beautiful," said Arthur as he munched on his cereal. "Simply beautiful."

Chapter Two

The Minister for Culture, Tezira Chelimo alighted from the car to a big applause from the crowd that had waited for almost five hours at the Boma grounds in the heart of Kapchorwa Town. The Boma Grounds doubled as the playing field of Kapchorwa Primary School and for every other important function in Kapchorwa. It was fairly strategic because it was near the centre of the one street town and close to Stanbic and Centenary Banks, the Town Council offices and the District Administration offices.

There is something about applauding crowds that boosts one's confidence and on this day, Madam Minister's confidence was particularly sky-high. She had on an ankle-length brightly colored two piece *kitenge* of green and red print. Green was the more dominant color. A single string of red African beads adorned her long neck and medium sized round earrings made from the same beads dangled from her ears. The fitting top of the outfit accentuated her curved waist. The skirt rolled on her hips down to her legs in a comfortable fit. It was not the sort of skirts which were so tight that the wearer could hardly walk making the bums look like they would tear it any moment in order to free themselves from the bondage. She had on low heeled red shoes and a marching red handbag made from those big beads only found in Kapchorwa. She always wore short hair. Although she wore no makeup, her skin was a silky shine.

"I am a soap and water woman," she would tell her friends who would groan with disgust accusing her of not being "dot com" compliant because she did not wear make-up.

She flashed a wide smile, showing gleaming white teeth, made even whiter by her dark gums and dark skin, typical of most Sabiny women. She raised her hand and waved from side to side, in politician style, acknowledging the cheers, pausing every so often to shake an outstretched hand here and there. Everybody wants to know how it feels to shake a minister's hand, her minister colleague had once told her.

As she made her way to the platform, the Emcee – a local councillor of some sort who sincerely believed that being councillor was no small thing – was outdoing himself announcing the arrival of the guest of honour, his voice booming over the gentle sound of the Kapchorwa Town Academy brass band that was playing a lively folk tune *Cemtaritit* – the one tune that when it is played, no Kapchorwans would stay seated. The Kapchorwans swung into dance action.

With a confidence born out of practice, the minister stood tall and elegant as the band struck up the national anthem. The crowds shuffled to their feet to show respect and patriotism.

But it is one thing to know the tune of the national anthem and a completely different kettle of fish to know how to sing it. You could literally count how many people knew the anthem well enough to sing it …

just a few folks, mostly those in the VIP tent. Even then, many of them were singing off-key.

Two or three chaps on the far side of the tent were humming along, but one could clearly see that they were not very sober. They sounded like a rusty old guitar being strummed out of tune. An old lady under the mango tree was either singing or grinning throughout the song, but either way showing her toothless gums.

A few old men, faces wrinkled and backs bent from years of toil in the garden were happy to watch silently through it all. In all their years of existence, they had never learnt to sing the national anthem, for the simple reason that visits from government officials on official occasions which would warrant singing of such songs had been few and far between over the years. Even then, the national anthem was written and sang in English, a language neither of them could be accused of knowing.

A few young fellows remained seated, content to simply raise their hands in respect of the national anthem but from the smirk on their faces it was clear that remaining on their seats was borne out of contempt than sheer necessity. It felt nice to be anti-establishment.

It was soon time for speeches – the most dreaded at any function; usually the time when those who simply came because they enjoyed brass band music or hoped to catch a glimpse of the big man – in this case, woman – take time off to grab a swig of banana juice or munch on a pancake. It was certain that most of them would not pay attention until the real speech began – the one from their home girl, the minister. They saw no reason to listen to the whole long line of speechmakers – the Local Council 1, then Local Council 2, up to the District Chairman, then other government officials who were regarded as important.

It had been a long ride from Kampala to Kapchorwa and clearly the guest of honour was tired. Matters were not helped by the fact that she had managed to snatch barely two hours of sleep the night before. She had to first finish reading through a pile of reports on cultural institutions then draft a report for the Prime-Minister, all that in just two days before she could proceed to Kapchorwa. And then her daughter Daisy had told her the day before that she had been having a constant throbbing headache and neither panadol nor any other painkiller, was helping. Her mother could not understand why. She had told the family doctor who advised that the girl should take plenty of water. These thoughts had made sleep escape from her tired body. She soon began dozing off, her head rolling first to one side, then to the other every after a few minutes as the monotonous drone of speeches continued.

A few smiles erupted across the tent as the minister's head drooled and dropped in turns. A group of naughty schoolboys in pink shirts and khaki trousers began betting a few coins each, on which way the minister's head would drop next. They soon went into excited giggles as with each turn of the head, some money was won.

The speechmakers, each eager to impress the minister were not aware that the object of their efforts had wandered off to slumberland. Fortunately the loud voice of the Emcee, a man who clearly presupposed that all the people had a hearing deficiency, jolted the minister awake.

"Madam Minister," he began. "Today is not a day for speeches."

That was after 10 speeches or so, which had lasted more than two hours in total. The irony was not lost on most people and a ripple of mirth broke out, lasting the better part of a minute. Even Madam Minister managed a tired smile that the Emcee took as an encouragement to attempt more humour. But just then he checked the clouds gathering quickly and ominously with promise of rain and decided against wasting any more time.

"So it is my pleasure with all humility to invite you, Madam Minister, to address your people."

The applause was deafening, as the mountain folks of Sabiny-land welcomed their girl who had done them proud by becoming a Minister. Chelimo, skilled in the art of public speaking, knew how to read the moods in crowds and come up with the appropriate rhetorical device to handle them.

"*Olei-yei*!!," she screamed in greeting.

"*Yei*!" the crowd screamed back.

"*Oleiiiiii-yeiiiii!*!" the Minister went again.

"*Yeiiiiiiiiiiiiiiiii*!!!!" the crowd, now worked up, chanted back. At the third *Olei-yei*, the crowd went crazy and the band, sensing the mood too, took full advantage and struck up a *Chekwoye*t – a generic name for circumcision tunes. This one was particularly lively and infectious. Although this was not *Wonset* or circumcision season, that was besides the point; this was celebration nevertheless. It was a good time to hear a *Chekwoyet* tune … and dance away they did.

The Sabiny know how to gig away; holding a monkey tail in hand and moving the hands up and down in rhythm with the song, as the legs provide some kind of scantily organized support. The dried tail belonged to the Colobus Monkey, also a resident of Kapchorwa, albeit in the forested areas for obvious reasons, and liked especially for its huge fur portfolio. It is the monkey tail that makes the dance special and creates an artificial attractiveness that the dance itself may inherently lack.

Chelimo had come with her own monkey tail and she bobbed up and down, trying to remain dignified, while at the same time dancing well, a dance whose first requirement was that all dignity and pretences thereto be put aside.

Over the years, the war in the Democratic Republic of Congo had considerably altered the equation for the Colobus Monkey. The influx of refugees from DRC into Uganda had brought with it new cuisines and strange appetites as the refugees spread across the country. Many of them settled in Kapchorwa where they enjoyed booming business in the tailoring field, stitching colorful *kitenge* materials that the Sabiny loved. It was when the

Congolese saw the monkey tails being used in the local dances that they inquired as to whether the owners of the tails were still in good supply around Kapchorwa.

The natives simply pointed at the mountain and that was it. The Congolese began to hunt down the monkeys, caring less about the tails and more about the meat. Soon the tails were in short supply as the monkey population decreased. It took the intervention of the Resident District Commissioner to make the Congolese let the monkeys be. He threatened the Congolese with repatriation if they did not check their appetites.

The Minister's speech was something nobody had anticipated. After the usual greetings, her first statement took them by surprise, especially as she skipped all the usual protocol niceties and hit the nail right on the head.

"My people of Kapchorwa, today I come with one message: that we must protect our girls and our women from the cruelty of the knife that deprives them of their true womanhood under the pretence of making them women."

The silence was more deafening than the applause had been. The thunderbolt that people expected to come from the gathering clouds above had come from right next to them. This is not what most of them had hoped for. There was no promise of roads and bridges; of jobs and schools. The storm to flee was not the one coming from above, it was this one coming from right here, whispered some of the old men and women.

"The time has come for the knife to return to its sheath, for our surgeons to return to their gardens. If they ever want to use the knife in their gardens no one will stop them. But to use it on our girls, let us all say no, no, no. not anymore."

Silence.

"I am here to tell you my people of Sebei; that the God who created us was no fool. He knew exactly what He was doing when He gave every woman the various parts on her body. Nobody has the right to remove any part of it."

At this point there were certainly quite a few dissenting voices that wanted to be heard but a quick look at the two pick-up trucks loaded with military policemen who seemed to be eager to oblige anyone who wanted a beating made them think twice. A few people, mostly elderly men and women shuffled away like chicken whose feathers had been ruffled by a superior cock.

"God created a woman full," she continued. "I want you to know that those who claim to be making her full by removing parts of her body that make her so, are instead making her less of a woman. My people, you all know how terrible some of the effects of female circumcision are. You all know that we have lost some gallant women of this land due to the practice. We have lost mothers. We have lost sisters. Yet we have continued to shield this evil," she went on in an unwavering voice. "Let us all say no to the knife!"

Timid murmurs began to emerge from among the young women in the crowd; but soon it gave way to a thunderous uproar. Some young men joined the young women.

"We say no! We say no! We say no!" the young people roared, throwing their arms in the air.

Madam Minister got excited about the response and she paused for effect and readiness, to deliver another bombshell. Just then her personal assistant came flying up the platform, phone in hand and jabbering animatedly. It was clear something was amiss or someone on the phone that this man was holding had something very important to say - something that could not wait.

It was not every day that a minister's speech is interrupted by a phone call. Even the President was known to hold his peace when it turned out that the minister he wanted was addressing a public rally. People looked at each other, wondering who could be so important that the minister's personal assistant who was known for his strict adherence to rules of procedure – one of the main reasons he was hired – had been quick to break them and had lost his composure - another rarity - in the process.

"Nicho you can please wait," the Minister said, leaning away from the microphone.

"No Madam," Nicho mumbled as he shook his head.

"You can wait," she repeated.

"Here," Nicho continued to shake his head as he came closer to the minister pushing the phone through to her.

"Are you mad?" the Minister hissed, unleashing her anger. Chelimo was known for her short temper sometimes.

"I am sorry madam, but it's urgent. It's State House calling … the … er … actually … His Excellency the President is on the line madam."

The Minister held her breath, sure something had gone wrong. Possibly very wrong. But again on second thoughts she decided this was a moment she could use to her advantage. It would not be a terribly bad idea to let people know that the President was in the habit of calling her from time to time – interrupting her meals, meetings and even important speeches such as the one she was delivering. She decided she would make the most of the opportunity, well aware of the important election just months away. She saw this as an opportunity to woo as many voters as possible.

"My people you will excuse me," she began, with a smug look on her face. "You will kindly excuse me. The President has something important to tell me." Another ripple swept across the pool, but this time one of admiration and gasps of excitement.

"The President is talking to our girl just like that!" A toothless old woman couldn't contain her excitement. The Minister turned away from the microphone and received the phone from Nicho.

"Yes, Your Excellency, ..." She trailed off and the smugness on her face disappeared. It was not the president but an unfamiliar voice, deep, calm and intimidating. It was obviously a man; one she didn't know, but from the voice, one she'd rather not know.

"This is not the President," a voice was saying calmly. He was in no hurry; he was clearly in charge and knew he had all the bargaining chips on his side of the table.

"You do not know me, but you will soon get to know me. You may call me Boss if you like...though I doubt you have much choice in the matter."

He was taking his time and the Minister, so used to giving orders had this chilling fear that it was her turn to take them and something deep inside her was suggesting she couldn't afford not to.

"I lead an important organization that seeks to uphold the pride of the Sabiny; the sovereignty of our people and the integrity of our culture. Our organization comprises of both men and women. We are fed up with this dangerous, stupid campaign that you are waging against our culture."

The Minister had been in the middle of an important speech when the phone call came and now she was right in the middle of another speech, except that this time she was not the one delivering it. She had turned into an unwilling audience.

"We shall not allow you to kill our values, to turn our women into prostitutes and unfaithful wives. To help you out of the way, we have, as I speak now, your daughter Daisy, in our hands, and we are going to do to her exactly what you are saying should no longer be done to our women. Do not bother contacting the police because you will never find us. You will hear from me again one of these good days. Oh, and I will preside over the cutting ceremony myself and send you a copy of what promises to be an excellent video.

"I believe it will be a gripping watch. You may want to look at it. And I have this feeling that you may want to keep as a memento, whatever we cut off her; so we'll send that too by special delivery. But do not worry about her safety. We are not killers and I mean it. We shall send your daughter back to you, safe and sound just a little bit less downstairs."

There was a pause, and Chelimo almost unable to breathe cut in.

"Wait please. Where are you? Let's talk," Chelimo was desperate. "I will give you any amount of money you want but please…"

He laughed, more like a hyena cackling away.

"We don't want your money. We are not after any ransom. We are respectable people of the tribe. And again, let me reassure you not to worry about your daughter. We will return her to you safe and sound after we have done exactly as we please. Stay well Madam Minister." The line went dead.

"Wait please. Please talk to me. Hello, hello!" Chelimo cried, clutching onto the phone like a life line. But she only heard the echo of her own voice.

"Oh God it can't be true, let it not be true," Chelimo half thought, half whispered. Then her legs buckled and she swayed for a moment. Nicho quickly held her.

"Madam, whatever it is, try to hold yourself together. People are staring." Chelimo looked at Nicho and she held onto him for strength.

"Tell them that the rally cannot go on. That the President has given me an urgent and extremely sensitive assignment," she told Nicho. Both Nicho and the bodyguard were now in panic, wondering what the President could have told their boss that upset her to that magnitude. Had he fired her from the cabinet?

Nicho managed to give her message to the mammoth gathering. There was a minute of silence as they stood perplexed and then broke out in simultaneous murmurs.

"You never know with these big offices. May be the President is sending our girl to go and talk to the Queen of England." Once again, the telephone call from the President affirmed their belief that the President had a lot of confidence in their girl. In her, they had voted well. They had voted wisely.

Within a few minutes, Chelimo had found her resolve. She quickly jumped into her car brushing aside her bodyguard who wanted to carry out the usual rituals of opening and closing the door and saluting. The driver was already igniting the engine.

"Where to Madam?"

"Drive as fast as you can even if it means flying the car," she screamed.

"To where Madam?" the driver asked, perplexed.

"Anywhere!" she shouted and then added, "Oh my God. Please God help me. Forgive me my trespasses, punish me as you deem fit Lord but let my baby not be mutilated."

"Madam, where are we going?" the driver's voice cut in.

"Just drive out of this place. And drive fast!" she barked.

"Madam, that's what I am doing but which direction should I take?"

"To the Police Station of course," Chelimo replied.

The driver turned madly around, tyres screeching. The police station was in the opposite direction.

*****

Chelimo jumped out of the car as soon as she reached the police station. Running, she went straight to the reception her bodyguard panting after her.

"Where is the District Police Commander's office?" she demanded without any pretence to preamble.

The receptionist, no doubt having a bad day, was not about to take this lying down.

"Woman, you just walk in, nay-run in and you think you can meet the DPC just like that? You think you are General Kahe the Inspector General of Police?" She looked at Chelimo, her eyes moving from head to the shoe-less feet and up again.

"Why don't you just do your job? I want the DPC!" Chelimo screamed

"This is the Minister of Culture," the bodyguard cut in, clearing his throat and stepping forward to take charge. "Please take us to the DPC's office quickly." The receptionist's jaw dropped. Then, embarrassed and wordless, she hastily led Chelimo down the corridor. Chelimo, bodyguard in tow, literally ran.

"There madam, room 23," the receptionist said. She then beat a hasty retreat, fearful that her silly indiscretion would attract a serious administrative sanction. Taking such liberty with a minister had not been a clever idea after all. Next time she'd be more careful; she decided that she had learnt a harsh lesson.

Chelimo pushed aside the two astonished guards outside the DPC's office and threw the door open.

"Sir, my daughter has been kidnapped. You must move now and find her."

The DPC stood up perplexed and annoyed with his guards for letting in a seemingly mad woman but he quickly adjusted his thinking when he saw a policeman close to her heels, obviously a bodyguard.

"What is going on?" The DPC asked as he put on his glasses.

The bodyguard stepped forward. "Sir, she is the Minister for Culture, Hon. Tezira Chelimo," he said.

"Of course. I am sorry." the DPC said. He saluted her and pulled out a chair.

"Bring something to drink - a bottle of water - quickly," he ordered one of the guards. He had now recognized her, having seen her in the papers a few times.

"Please just find my daughter."

"Madam, was she kidnapped from here in Kapchorwa? And when was this?"

"The kidnappers called me awhile ago saying they already have her. So it's now like half an hour ago since they ki – kid – kidna -"

"Okay, okay madam, from where?"

"I have no idea," she responded.

"Did they ask you for money? Ransom?"

"No." Chelimo told him everything they had told her.

The DPC's hand shuffled into his pocket and he extracted a black Nokia mobile phone and started dialling as he moved out.

Chelimo stood up and followed him.

"Who are you calling?" She shrieked. "I hope not the police. Please don't call the police. The kidnappers said I shouldn't call the police or go to them," she shouted almost grabbing the DPC's phone. The DPC calmly assured her that he'd do nothing of the sort.

"You are at church informing the priests," he thought wryly to himself, although he understood her plight. Years of experience had taught him to smell a tight spot from a mile away: this was such a one. He slipped into another room and dialled the number of the Inspector General of Police.

"Sir, this is the DPC Kapchorwa. It's a red button emergency. The daughter of the Minister of Culture has been kidnapped by people who say they want to circumcise her because her mother, the Minister, is preaching against female circumcision."

*****

The IGP gripped his handset. This was a red button emergency indeed.

"So where is the minister?" the IGP asked.

"Right here in my office, sir. She is in tatters, so to speak," the DPC declared as if he was unveiling a great scientific discovery. The IGP felt like hurling his phone at him for the stupid pronouncement.

"Let me speak to her."

The DPC quickly moved towards the minister and gave her the phone.

"Honourable Minister, this is the Inspector General of Police. Sorry for what has happened but I am sure we will arrest the situation. How long ago did this take place?"

"Not very sure. Maybe about half an hour ago. As soon as the goons called, I drove here immediately. IGP, you must find my daughter. You must get her before those people ccirc...circ...cuu-muti-mutii-mutilate her. Please, please, will you do it?"

It was half a plea, half a command.

"Madam, we will do everything possible to see that your daughter is safe," replied the IGP.

"I asked; will-you-do-it? I did not ask whether there was a possibility that it could be done. You sound cautious and cagey. What I want from you now is a straight answer," she commanded.

The IGP sighed and almost told her that in their trade, there are never any straight answers. Only possibilities and keeping the flame of hope burning. But time was of essence.

"I need to get the most current photograph of your daughter."

"Drive straight to my house in Ntinda. They will give it to you."

"What is her full name?"

"Daisy Chemtai Twino."

"How old is she?"

"Almost thirteen."

"Thank you madam. Now, a helicopter will bring you to Kampala immediately," the IGP said.

"Do you think they have ha-haa-harmed my baby?" She could feel her heart pounding in her chest, as if in an effort to rip open the rib cage.

"Hon. Minister, don't worry. Everything is under control;" the IGP said in a strong hopeful voice, trying to reassure her. But the Minister knew that such situations could sometimes be tricky.

"As you know madam, in such cases, time is of essence. So please proceed to the helicopter to bring you back to Kampala. The DPC will do everything that needs to be done that end. We shall be waiting for you." The line went off.

The DPC stood up and asked the Minister to go with him. They moved out of the police headquarters quickly and quietly. The only noise was that of the policemen's heavy shoes on the gravel and the sudden eruption of some loud voice on his walkie-talkie.

The distinctive whoosh sound of the chopper's twin rotor blades rotating in quick-fire motion as they approached the police airwing affair parked at the far end of the football field, half a mile away from the police station, told the story of a pilot who'd been already warned that there was an emergency flight afoot and he'd better make it snappy.

His engine was properly warmed, very much ready for the flight. Soon they were airborne.

*****

Chapter Three

The Inspector General of Police's office was on the tenth floor of the imposing building that housed the senior staff of the Police Force. The IGP had chosen the topmost floor because it gave him a commanding view of the entire city. He always reached his office by 5:00 a.m. and would spend some time looking out from the four windows of the office as if surveying and spying on the city as it stirred to life, looking for any trouble spots. It was whispered by the junior staff that it was at this hour that he was most alert. His small eyes set in a long face would dart here and there as he scratched his close shaven head and paced up and down in deep thought. This was his daily ritual.

He was a tall, pencil-thin man, whose sheer dedication to hard work was cult-like. He had managed the almost impossible feat of bringing Kampala city to law and order in a period where uncalled for riots had been the order of the day. The crime rate had also come down. The IGP was well known for his firm stand on cracking down crime. In the same breath, he was also reputed to possess a large heart with a bounty of humaneness.

On this Tuesday morning, he had given a sigh of relief because no serious incidents of crime had so far been reported. He had settled down to do office work till late afternoon only for his calm to be disturbed by that call from the DPC of Kapchorwa.

As soon as he finished giving instructions to the DPC to have the Minister of Culture flown to Kampala, he pressed the intercom that sat on his desk.

"Yes sir?" his Secretary's voice whispered from the other side.

"Convene a High Level Meeting in my Board room in ten minutes." He then proceeded to list who he wanted at the meeting. "The Director Generals of Internal and External Security, the Director Crime Investigation Department, the Director, Anti-Terrorism Squad, the Commander of the Flying Squad, the Special Force Commander, the Chief of Military Intelligence, the Permanent Secretaries of Ministries of Defence, Internal Affairs, Security and the Deputy Chief of Defence Forces plus the Chief Controller of Traffic."

"Yes sir," the secretary said as his line went dead. He paced up and down the room, scratching his head, stopping to look out of the window as many times as he paced around. As quickly, he turned to the phone and pressed the intercom again.

"And the Commander of the Alpine Brigade."

Kapchorwa was a mountainous place and he was very sure the kidnappers were going to take the girl there. That's where the Alpine Brigade would come in handy.

He resumed his pacing up and down, occasionally stopping at his desk to jot something down in the notepad. He was anxious to get to the bottom of the kidnap as soon as he could. Times like this could make or break an individual. There would be flowers and promotions if all went well. But failure could be a harbinger of doom. There could be a major reshuffle in the force. And such reshuffles had the bad history of carrying with them, the heads of the forces. He swallowed hard and pressed the intercom as a chill went down his spine.

"Have you got everybody?"

"Yes sir."

"Good. Make sure the boardroom is ready."

"Okay sir."

The Secretary fidgeted with files on her desk and sighed, "It's as if the country is on the brink of war! It's been a while since boss summoned the high level security apparatus!" She wondered aloud before fumbling with her phone to call people at the Chelimo residence to ask for the recent picture of the daughter.

Meanwhile, the security chiefs were all asking themselves the same question as they worried about how they could beat the maddening traffic jam in order to be at the IGP's office in the stipulated ten minutes. Even with a lead car, it was sometimes impossible to manoeuvre through the jam and the undisciplined drivers, cyclists and *bodaboda* (motorcycle taxis) all competing for space.

Amazingly, they all made it within the ten minutes and the Secretary directed them to the boardroom. She quickly buzzed the IGP.

"Sir, they are all here."

"Good," he said as he marched to the boardroom.

"The Minister of Culture's daughter has been kidnapped," he started.

These were seasoned officers, used to all sorts of emergencies and frightful situations. Nobody raised an eyebrow or expressed shock. They listened, their notebooks open and pens poised.

"She was kidnapped about forty five minutes or an hour ago, as she entered their residence in Ntinda. The girl is twelve to thirteen years. Mother was away on duty in Kapchorwa. Kidnappers say they want to circumcise the girl because her mother is preaching against female circumcision. We must find the girl before the savages do anything to harm her."

"Kidnappers are usually very smart people. Maybe the girl is still around Kampala. Maybe they have hidden her in a place which they think we may not suspect until they are convinced that security agencies are looking elsewhere for her. Alternatively, after kidnapping her, they must have changed cars because they initially kidnapped her off in the minister's car. They know it is too risky to take her in that car. So they will in all probability dump the minister's car somewhere, put her in another and straight away drive most likely to Kapchorwa. That is where the Minister comes from. It is most probable that the kidnappers will want to torment the minister by taking the girl to the environment that fits in with the cultural norms of the people she is preaching against."

He paused for effect as he cracked his knuckles, a habit that usually rubbed his subordinates the wrong way, irritating them to the core. But they were also aware that the boss always broke into his knuckle cracking when the situation at hand was complex.

"To describe the kidnap of the Minister's daughter as complex would be an understatement," he continued. "I know that the whole country is going to be gripped with fear and anxiety. The country is going to literally hold its breath. I know how these people operate."

"So what do we do Chief?" asked SSP Teko who the whole force knew enjoyed the confidence of the IGP.

"That's why we are here. To find out exactly what we should do," the IGP snapped at Teko as if to say instead of proposing the way forward you are leaving everything to me as if I am God.

There was a moment of silence only broken by SSP Bob's heavy breathing. SSP Bob ate far too much, munching away at everything that came his way and filling his stomach with huge chunks of animal protein every lunch time. He always ended the day with his evening beer. Vegetables never knew his plate. "I am not an animal to eat grass," he always declared with unconcealed contempt.

It was a wonder that he could even climb the stairs to the IGP's office. In spite of his lifestyle-induced diseases, he possessed a sharp intellect and could unravel complex cases in a remarkable manner. In his waking moments, he could give an answer to a riddle that had defeated everybody.

The IGP turned to his second in command.

"Give orders to all the police stations along the Kampala-Kapchorwa highway to immediately erect roadblocks each at a ten kilometre distance. Spread them to cover every route which can be used in the same direction. We can't afford to leave anything to chance. Make sure that within those ten-kilometre distances, there are plain clothed security men to detect any suspicious behaviour. Make sure that at every roadblock, all the vehicles occupants are made to get out for a thorough check. Stop every vehicle. I repeat, every vehicle, including ministerial and other government vehicles. Stop ambulances as well. I mean, every vehicle must be stopped," he paused as he noticed frowns on some faces.

He then blurted out angrily, "Do not frown. How many times have you seen an ambulance speeding, with sirens screaming only to stop at some house and charcoal is offloaded?" There was a moment of silence.

"For that matter, let us do our job with no exceptions. And those *bodabodas*; stop every one of the those chaotic motorbikes and check the passengers," he paused as he got out a photograph of the young girl and handed it to the CID Chief to pass around.

"That's the girl. Within five minutes, make sure all police officers manning the roadblocks have got a picture of this young girl."

"But how chief? We are not magicians!"

"I know. Send it on their phones. Thank God for technology."

He looked at the copy which he had put in his wallet and gritted his teeth in anger.

"This could be my ten year old daughter!" He swore quietly. He pushed the picture back in the pocket as his eyes narrowed dangerously.

All this time, everybody had kept quiet.

"We do not yet have any information about the physical appearance of the kidnappers, so let's concentrate on looking for the girl. The CID Chief should deploy in all the corners of the city. Start with the Minister's house. You know what information to look for. Interview all the people who stay there." The IGP went on to give each Security Chief a brief of what they should do.

"Any questions?"

Teko's hand shot up.

"Yes?" the IGP pointed at Teko.

"Sir, where is the Minister?"

"On her way from Kapchorwa."

"Any other question?"

There was silence.

"Now everybody beat it. Everybody to their particular duty and remember, silence," said the IGP putting his fingers to his lips. "You all must be aware that we are dealing with hardcore criminals. Silence is paramount."

He got out his notebook and begun to scribble furiously as the team streamed out of his office.

"Bwana Teko!" the IGP called out after the officers.

"Yes sir!" Teko answered as he opened the door to the IGP's office again.

"Go direct to the Minister's house and wait for her there. Once she enters, she is not to move out, whatever the temptation might be. Understand?"

"Yes sir."

"These are hardcore criminals who can do anything to her."

"I understand sir."

"I hope so," replied the IGP sounding like he didn't believe that Teko understood.

Teko had already been told where the Minister's residence was. He chuckled as he moved out of the IGP's office.

"What's so funny?" asked the Flying Squad Commander who always spoke as if he was angry all the time.

"I am just amused by the IGP telling us to keep quiet about the kidnap. Is there any secret in this place? Within a short time, the whole thing will be on all the FM stations and social media. Keep quiet my foot! I mean it's not the village milkman's daughter who has been kidnapped for Christ's sake! It is a whole minister's daughter!"

The IGP pressed the intercom .

"Sir?" the secretary's voice came on

"Ask my ADC to come quickly."

The ADC stepped in immediately. It was as if he had been waiting for the instruction.

"I had told the top security officers to make sure nobody talks about this matter," the IGP stated as soon as his ADC entered. "But I have changed my mind. Make sure within ten minutes all the media outlets both print and electronic have this news. Most of the newspapers will print an early edition as soon as they get the news and the photograph of the girl. Get a new cell phone number and publicise it. Tell the public that that's the IGP's hotline and anybody with any information about the kidnapped girl should call that number. Receive every call no matter how idiotic the caller sounds. Understood?"

"Yes sir," the ADC said saluting.

After making sure that everything was moving according to plan, and all the officers were at their locations, the IGP settled to attend to other issues that awaited his attention. A few hours to close of day, he gave orders to his Chief body-guard to get his transport ready. He literally run out of his office, the two body-guards following suit. One of them quickly pressed the button for the lift but the IGP was already sprinting down the steps. The two guards run after him but they were not as agile as he was despite their being younger than he was and presumably more fit.

"We are heading to Ntinda. Step on the gas," he barked at his driver.

"Yes sir".

It did not take them long to reach the upscale Ministers' Village. The house was already surrounded by policemen looking ominous with their helmets. Chelimo had already arrived from Kapchorwa. Her household huddled in different spaces, their cheeks cupped in palms. They spoke in low whispers.

The Minister sat alone in a sofa near the door. She had exhausted all the questions she had been having on how her dear Daisy had been kidnapped. Over and over again, she had asked the same questions to almost everybody. To her family and neighbours, it was, did you see what happened? Were you all at home? How did it happen? And on and on. To others, it was what do you think happened? What do you think they are going to do to her? Do you think they need a ransom? And on and on. To the security, do you think you will find her? You will find her, wont you? She will be safe. Don't you think so? They won't hurt her, don't you think so? And on and on... Her lips now moved constantly but no word came out. .

The IGP opened the living room door and entered the modestly furnished, neat house. He saluted the Minister.

"Have you found my baby?" Chelimo cried out as she looked at the IGP with expectant eyes.

"No Madam. But we are on the move. The search is on."

Her eyes fell with utter dejection and disappointment.

"I am here so that we set off for Kapchorwa," the IGP was saying to the motionless form. "I am almost one hundred percent sure that they will take her to Kapchorwa to ...."

"Please don't say it!" Chelimo broke out in agony.

"Sorry Madam. I understand. I have organized a private car for you. It will take the lead and I will be directly behind you."

Chelimo also knew that time was of essence and she got up.

"But before we leave Madam, I am sorry but... I need to find out something."

"What do you need that I have not explained?"

"Aaah...It's just that...aaah..."

"Ask your questions. There are no more secrets in this matter."

"Do you still remember the date and month when it was done to you?"

"The what?"

The IGP looked away as he asked the question.

"I am sorry but... are you... were you circumcised?"

"Of what relevance is that to the circumstances if I am circumcised or not?" the minister almost shouted. The answer was loud and clear.

"Do you remember the month when you were circumcised?"

"How can I ever forget?" she said, her eyes narrowing to a small slit. Her voice was low, bitter and deliberate.

"Circumcision is carried out every month of December of each even year. This week - I don't recall the exact date - will be thirty three years since I was cut," she answered.

"And do you recall the exact location where this was done from?"

"But of course I do," she said with irritation as she entered the private car that the IGP had ready for her.

"IGP, just a minute sir," Teko called almost in a timid voice. The IGP halted in his stride.

"Talk." His lips quivered.

"Boss, I have an inkling why you took an interest in the timing and place......"

"Your inkling is right. The people we are dealing with are not dumb. They are smart. Professionals or whatever type. They want to exert revenge on the Minister. They will most probably want to rub it in - do unto the daughter at the same time and place as it was done unto the mother."

"Boss, that means we have only a short time within which to find the girl!"

"Get moving then."

Teko broke out in a cold sweat. The IGP was already in the car giving instructions to the driver as Teko quickly jumped in and the car sped off.

"Boss, why didn't we take the helicopter?"

"And alert those goons that we are in the area? Move!" he ordered the driver who did not need much prompting.

"You," the IGP barked at the driver. "Think you are driving a bridal couple?"

"I am sorry sir."

"Then show that you are not driving newlyweds."

And indeed the driver successfully proved that he was driving the cream of the Police force on a rescue mission. Chelimo's private car followed at a safe distance. The IGP had told the traffic chief about the private car in which the Minister was travelling. Just then, a voice came through the radio call.

"Sir, this is ADC Paul here," he began with excitement.

"This better be good news Paul," the IGP growled. "I have had enough bad news in these last few hours to take me through the rest of this year. Talk," the IGP ordered as if he was speaking to the ADC face to face.

When the ADC began talking, the IGP grabbed his cell phone to issue instructions to his case in-charge.

"The Minister's car has been found in Gayaza, six kilometers from the city."

"But you are not saying anything about the most important point: the whereabouts of the girl who had been on board!" the IGP barked and gave instructions on his other cell phone.

Within a few minutes, the head of Crime Scene Investigations (CSI) from police headquarters who the IGP had dispatched to Gayaza called back.

"That was quick."

"Yes sir."

"Aha?"

"We were already on the alert and so we just..."

"That's not why you called."

"Sir, there are no new finger prints on the car apart from those of the regular driver and the little girl."

The IGP switched him off.

"This is useless information," he said, his eyes concentrating on the car that carried the minister.

As Chelimo sat back in the car, fear, worry, anxiety and anger were written all over her face. She was on a journey back to her homeland surrounded by policemen and security operatives of all types on a mission to make sure her daughter Daisy did not undergo circumcision. As she was being driven on this journey to rescue her daughter, her mind went on another journey, many years back, when she went through what her daughter must never go through. What no woman should ever go through…

Chapter Four

Chelimo had fond memories of the first twelve years of her childhood. She grew up in a typically rural homestead surrounded by love from her parents, siblings and all the other members of her clan. Everything was smooth sailing. School was good albeit the agony they sometimes had to undergo courtesy of the teacher's cane. But one could avoid it by not being late for school or by not talking in class while the lesson was going on. Life was good and full of happiness then.

Then everything turned into a nightmare the year she made thirteen. What was about to happen was whispered loudly in school. It was time for those not yet circumcised to face the knife. Months soon rolled by and it was third term - running from August to mid-December. The cutting would take place as soon as the December holidays commenced.

Chelimo had heard all there was to hear about circumcision. The rituals before the cutting, the terrible pain during the cutting and the aftermath which was nothing to write home about. She lived in fear and trepidation of the upcoming knife and she was not the only one. Often times, the girls would tell of how scared they were. They would whisper to each other when they thought no one was hearing. Sometimes they would talk about it openly. This was however always dismissed by the elderly women as rumours. "The pain is bearable." The old women would lie. "After this, you will be a real woman of the hills of Kapchorwa. Until you are cut, you are just a child. It is the knife which will make you a real woman. It is the knife which will expose you to the secrets of our land."

"*Eyo*," she started, her heart pounding. Her mother sighed. She knew that every time her daughter called her mother in their language, the issue to be discussed would be very serious.

"Yes my child?"

"Can't I escape this thing?" she asked as tears sprung into her eyes.

"No my child. It is something you cannot escape. You have to go through it. I did and so did your grandmother and your great grandmothers. Child, don't worry. All will be well. As you go through it, know that I will be there by your side even though you will not see me in the flesh. I'll be standing with you, connecting with you and reaching out to you. I will give you the courage to go through it proudly."

Again she sighed and looked far into space, spending a little while in deep reflection before she resumed.

"Child it is our fate, it is our lot as women. That is how it is supposed to be and we have to accept it. In life, some things are like that. But it is also our pride because we are not cowards. Some tribes have cowardly women. We are not cowards." she ended on a militant note, lips pouting, fists clenched and forehead creased in defiance. Then Chelimo knew she had no choice.

*****

One very early morning the following December, as the *Wonset* season kicked off, Chelimo heard the sharp whistles of the young girls who had come to pick her. Her heart in her mouth, she jumped from her bed. Within no time, her mother was by her side.

"Child," she whispered as she embraced her. "Do not fear. All will be well," her mother said as she untied the kanga cloth she always wrapped around herself and wrapped it around Chelimo. "You will need this."

Chelimo kept quiet, a tremor of fear ripping through her bowels. When she looked at her mother, she could tell that mother understood what her daughter was going through. The whistle and thud of stamping feet was now at their door. Mother took daughter by the hand and slowly led her to the door which she opened. "We, the mothers will join you later," her mother whispered. She pressed her hand firmly and then gently handed her over to the merry girls chanting away. This gave Chelimo some hope, knowing that her mother would be there.

There was renewed whistle blowing and stamping of feet as they welcomed Chelimo into the middle of the circle they had formed in front of the house. As she joined the group, she felt like she had just been swallowed up. The ululation was deafening. One of the girls put a whistle in Chelimo's mouth and beckoned her to blow it. Chelimo held the whistle between her lips and she blew away the thoughts that were threatening to choke her. The crowd danced in recognition of her whistle and they moved on to other candidates' homes.

Within no time, Chelimo was also stamping her feet to the rhythm of the other girls. She tried to look back to see if her mother was still standing on the veranda but one of the girls whispered to her;

"Don't look back. It will bring you bad luck. Once you join the group, there is no looking back."

Chelimo fell back into the line of the dancing girls. That was just the beginning of so many ceremonies as she later realised. She knew all the girls were as scared as she was but there was comfort in numbers and in the frenzied music. *Wonset* was in the air.

*****

A cyclist dashed by at full speed, tree branches strapped to the bike and sweeping the road sending clouds of dust up in the air.

He was the fore runner. His appearence signalled the beginning of the real action.

The fore runner led the girls and they soon arrived at the venue. Their faces were different; they had changed completely. They were very rude and tough; angry with everything around them. They were in a bad mood – just ripe for *rotwet* – the knife. The circumcision spot was an open ground and the *cemerik* - candidates for circumcision, found that it had been covered with sheets of polythene. Chelimo was a trifle apprehensive, not sure whether she would go through it calmly. But her best friend Chemtai was a different spirit. She talked throughout, encouraging the other girls and reminding them that this was the time to cross the bridge. Although some girls were filled with trepidation at the prospect of going through the pain and achieve the sizeable feat of not flinching or appearing to do so, Chemtai was the exact opposite: *rotwet* couldn't come soon enough, as far as Chemtai was concerned.

Here, they were led in a different kind of wild dance each of the *cemeriyandet* – circumcision candidate - was carrying a *Sayendet* – a dried tail of the colobus monkey. It made the dance more colourful. Months before the circumcision season, Chelimo, had had to hunt for her own monkey and get a tail, like every other *cemeriyandet.* It was a sign of bravery for one to hunt down a monkey on their own.

At the circumcision grounds, the dancing was hot and wild; the drumbeat strong and inviting. The whistles were kind of off-key, completely out of pitch with the voices, but the people's spirits weaved in with the rhythm-less rhythm. It was a kind of tonic syncopation, sounding a bit weird but certainly nothing out of line, in the circumstances. When they finally lay down, they were told that the legs had to be wide apart, eyes staring at the sky without blinking. Anybody who blinked would be labelled a coward - they would use it against her for the rest of her life as a coward who couldn't withstand *rotwet.* Each *cemeriyandet* remained with their hands up straight, one hand holding the dancing tail which they were told not to put down until the knife had come and gone. Some of the onlookers were cheeky and stubborn and they teased the girls, calling them cowards and idiots. The girls could not respond - not a word, otherwise one would attract the crack of a whip from the escorts. Real women were not supposed to talk anyhow or respond to insult, no matter how strong the provocation.

*****

Chelimo remembered also that before the D-day the candidates had had several days of movements which was part of the *kurset* – the invitation dance for circumcision celebrations. Each *cemerik*, fully clad in the circumcision regalia (head gear, monkey tail, whistle and a cloth tied at the back) was required to traverse the land, inviting all known relatives to the circumcision celebrations. The relatives offered them gifts such as goats, cows, money, hens and much more. These gifts were not for sheer love; they were necessities that would help them meet expenses of the circumcision process.

Chelimo did not have too many relatives; but Chemtai, quite a handful of a young woman, did not only have many relatives, but even more close friends who seemed to stick with her more than her own relatives. That also meant that there was no end of places to visit and after seven days, Chelimo thought she'd collapse. But she was also aware that this dancing was nothing compared to the bigger job of facing the *rotwet*, which lay ahead.

On the day before circumcision, the *cemeriandet* were gathered for the final dancing. Apart from the regular gear, the girls wore *kanga* cloths or strips of cloth from their mothers. The girls respected their mothers because all the mothers were circumcised. These were women who did not cry when they were circumcised. Each girl knew she had the strength of her mother because it was no use inheriting cowardice.

By mid-afternoon of circumcision eve, every *cemerik* girl was fully decorated with colourful lines on their faces and all over their bodies. There were all ready for the occasion. They wore brightly coloured dresses and *kangas* and as they swayed their small hips, the colours formed amazing patterns. They indeed looked beautiful but in a wild kind of way. But it was this that distinguished them as candidates for the knife. Old women went to work furiously: two sheep were slaughtered; and their blood and dung were mixed with white soil from the cliff and smeared on the faces of each *cemerik*. This was for appeasing the spirits lest they frown on the ceremony. If that happened, things could easily go wrong: a *cemerik* could fail to heal or they could even die. But all these things happened in silence. It was taboo to talk about this sacred ritual of circumcision. The girls were told that if they talked, the spirits could get annoyed and cause one to run mad, or get frustrated with bad luck and missed opportunities and fall short of the blessings of the tribe. They were told that if they talked, they could easily wake up on a fine morning and commit suicide just like that. It was therefore unheard of for anyone to defy the spirits. And so, secrecy prevailed. As a result, no disaster had ever befallen anyone in living memory and folks were anxious to keep it that way.

During circumcision preparations, it was a requirement that the *cemerik* would visit each others' homes on the eve of circumcision, to consolidate team spirit. That also meant that they would eat in each others' homes. At the entrance of each home, two spears would be put together in the form of an arching entrance. A sheep was squeezed and strangled to death with a blanket. Its intestines were then emptied of dung which was smeared on the candidates' faces as they entered. After the meal and the dancing, the *maturyondet* would ask them to regroup and continue to the next home. She would be the one to handle the lamp and direct the proceedings. Chelimo's *Bunda* was comprised of 20 girls, which meant that there were 20 or so meals through the night. The girls needed all the strength they could possibly get to face the knife. And with all the vigorous dancing, no food could stay too long in the stomach. The vigorous dancing was paramount in keeping the girls away from dangerous thoughts and tension. As the girls sat, legs forward, plates of food were handed to them: rice, matooke, millet, meat, and much more. They ate in silence. It was cold, but nobody dared complain. Anyone, foolhardy enough to do so would be asked to hand over the *sayadent*, and go away. She would be called a fool and other derogatory words such as stupid. Chemtai was certainly having a problem staying quiet, but she tried her best.

Amidst the dancing that punctuated most of the night, all manner of reckless talk and all manner of obscenity was permitted both among the *cemariandet* and the general public. It was the only time it was allowed anyway. Anything profane spoken outside this context and outside the marriage bed would be frowned upon by the community. But as was the case with such ceremonies, a lot of other things happened in the sidelines. Young men eloped with people's daughters. Marriage was a simple process - whisk the girl off to your home, keep her there for a few days and you'd be considered man and wife. There was not much fret and fuss about it. Later on, the parents of the girl would send a demand for bride price which would then be paid at an agreed time. Even girls who were ordinarily restricted got a chance to go out to the function. Circumcision was a community ceremony not a private affair. Some young men and women would not return home innocent, as the long night provided opportunity for forbidden intimacy. Students always looked forward to the December holiday when circumcision would take place. It was a God-sent opportunity to ease the tension built up in school.

Each *cemerik* was put in the care of a *maturyodent*- a mentor – that helped instruct them in dancing and on all rituals to be performed. Each *maturyondet* was confirmed to have undergone the circumcision ritual in order for them to be able to pass on the right knowledge and information to the girls. They were expected to coach their charges in the way that left nothing to chance. They were also expected to keep an eye on their charges lest any developed cold feet and decided to flee from the ritual..

Chemtai's *maturyondet* was having endless problems with her especially as Chemtai, wild as ever, insisted on dancing her own way. The poor old woman tired and exasperated, slapped her hard ordering her to fall into step with the others.

Chemtai then shocked everyone when she paused, walked nonplussed to the old woman and smacked her hard across the face.

"Nobody beats Chemtai!" she barked. "Never do it again."

The poor old woman stopped in her tracks. Everyone else paused in the song-singing. It was the oldest *maturyondet* who calmed matters down and reminded the cemeriandet that it was taboo to slap a mentor. The spirits would not be happy. "Please do not do it again," the *maturyondet* advised.

"And I'm not happy either," declared Chemtai, eyes flashing dangerously.

The leader of the *maturyondet* declared that there was far too much at stake to be compromised by the insolence of a cheeky little kitten. The spirits would contend with her. The ceremonies continued, even though the cemeriandet were shaken a little bit and it was clear the mentors had had their feathers really ruffled - this was completely without precedent. Nobody had ever thought anyone would - or could - cross a sacred line. Clearly, Chemtai did not think like the rest of her people.

As night fell, a *ntiliwet* - a creeper that grew on the mountainside – was tied around the big toe of the right foot of each *cemerik*. It was believed that the creeper would strengthen them and remove all creeping fear. Through the night, the girls received plenty of education on how to manage the family - including the critical matters of relating with in-laws, children, husbands and neighbours. Eating habits and general social etiquette expected of the quintessential Sabiny housewife were discussed. A wife was not allowed to come close to her father in-law or step in the same room with him. Serving him food was done through the children. She was not allowed to shake hands with him. Greeting a father-in-law was done from several meters away and in the politest way possible. On the other hand, a wife was encouraged to feel free with her mother in-law; after all, she was her mother as well. She was allowed to shake hands with the brothers to her husband, but was expected to show immense respect.

Another mentor talked long about the type of food that a wife would prepare to ensure that her husband's heart would not stray to other women. The last mentor talked about endurance and patience in marriage.

"This is a tough world and you should be strong," she said. "But if you can withstand the pain of *rotwet*- as I expect each one of you to, you need not be afraid of anything else in the world. No challenge will ever be too strong for you."

The girls listened steadfastly but when the subject of sexual relations came up, most of them who had never had carnal knowledge of any man looked down shyly while Chemtai and a few others who knew their way around giggled excitedly amongst themselves and had to be reminded from time to time to shut up.

"Be ready whenever your husband needs you," the woman said. "It is your duty to be available whenever he is in need. And always be faithful; it is taboo for a married woman to give herself to another man."

The final lecture was on what to do in the moment of circumcision. Yapsiwa, a sweet old soul who had taken hundreds of *cemariandet* through these ceremonies was giving final instructions. Yapsiwa had a few teeth missing but in a stretch of humour insisted that she had not yet reached the level of eating liver like a child; she still had plenty of bite to pick on a few bones. "There are four types of circumcision," Yapsiwa said. "But only one of them belongs to us."

She explained that the first type, only the prepuce- the fold of skin that covers the top of the clitoris is cut in a curve–like shape around the clitoral hood. The clitoris is exposed but not touched. The labia is not touched.

"A cowardly form of circumcision," she said dismissively, with a wave of hand in disgust. "It is too mild; just slight pain and a bit of bleeding. Some of our relatives like it too, but I think out of ignorance, because it actually makes a woman unfaithful instead. The second type, she explained, involved cutting the prepuce, clitoris and labia completely, while the third featured excision of all external genitalia plus stitching to narrow the vaginal entrance, leaving only a small opening for urine and menstrual blood. The narrow entrance is broken into at the time of marriage.

"The fourth category," said Yapsiwa, "includes all other operations piercing, stretching, burning and scratching or whatever. Not worth discussing now, I wonder why they even bother. The third category is for some of our friends in other parts of Africa- as our men may find no time or patience to begin looking for a hammer to break the door open," she said, as the girls laughed. "It is the second one instead that we have found more suitable, one that has served the Sabiny marriages to their best."

Chelimo remembered that at that time her hand had subconsciously wandered down to her groin. She had found herself touching her genitalia thinking about the fact that it was the last day on which she would last have her genitalia whole. The voices of the women had tapped her back on course.

"We shall expect you to lie on your back, legs wide open," Yapsiwa continued, her voice breaking the flow of Chelimo's thoughts. "The *mutik* has no time to begin opening your legs and then looking for the highway to cut the trees that line its side. Your duty is to look up at the sky and wait for the *rotwet*."

"Neither a twinge nor a tear is expected of you when *rotwet* touches you," cautioned the old woman. "Or else everyone will spit at you, you will be a social outcast," she warned, jabbing a long scrawny finger at the *cemeriandet.* "Then we shall marry you off to a toothless old man as a third or fourth wife- not a fine, strong young man- lest the children inherit your cowardice."

In spite of the tension, the *cemariandet* managed to laugh heartily as the thought of sharing a bed with a grandfather rather than a young man crossed their minds. Someone cheekily inquired as to what exactly Yapsiwa meant by 'toothless' and those who caught her drift laughed even louder. The naughty humour helped ease the tension further.

The crowing of the first cock in the night was a signal that it was time to descend to the Cheseber River, at Kapteret. The girls were clad in traditional circumcision gear with nothing underneath. There was no place for panties - they would not need panties for a long time.

It was a very cold morning but the dancing around the village had shaken off most of it. Chelimo was covered up in a mixture of fear, excitement and anticipation of what would happen after the river.

Her mentor led her into the river, naked. The mentor's experienced hands began to move all over her private parts, washing them elaborately. It felt awkward the woman's wrinkled and rough hands touching and washing her private parts which no one else had ever touched except when she was a small girl. It was then her mother who touched her and then taught her how to wash.

The action had begun. Nobody was allowed to watch this, so there were no spectators except the parents.

Other spectators would wait for them at the actual cutting ceremony later on.

The candidates emerged from the river trotting and dancing and waving their *Mongeshet* tails. They all looked like they were possessed. They were led to the chosen spot where they threw themselves backwards in a very athletic fashion. They were not supposed to sit down first and then gently lay themselves down. That was for children and tired old women, nobody was allowed to try and support herself - that was unfitness and cowardice; such a one was not woman enough to face the knife. They fell on their backs, a motion that sent their skirts flying up exposing their nakedness.

The mentors stepped forward, carrying cloth bags loaded with assorted herbs which only the circumcisers were familiar with. The secrets were guarded and kept by all. Those were secrets of the river. The instructions to each *cemerik* were firm, loud and clear: whatever you see here stays here. It was a curse to disclose to other people any information related to these herbs. It was a tight hush-hush passed from generation to generation. Whoever violated this sacred trust would hang herself, it was said. The mentors also carried millet flour to apply to the vagina. What was known and did not have to be kept secret was that the herbs together with the millet flour caused a sensitive reaction to the vagina, making the labia and the clitoris to fill and rise and point upwards. The flour also helped reduce the slipperiness of the organs to enable the mentor to hold them well for the surgeon to cut.

Chelimo's *maturyondet* was not happy with her charge, who kept telling her that her legs were not opened wide enough. The mentor pried her legs further open, chiding her for "keeping the legs together."

"You will only put your legs together after *rotwet* has come and gone," she reminded her.

Chelimo didn't agree but unlike her best friend Chemtai, she managed to keep her opinion to herself.

From a bag at her side, the mentor extracted the herbs and flour. Chemtai who seemed to know everyone and everything had already briefed Chelimo about the ordeal of the herbs. "The pain of the herbs is twice as much as that of the knife," she had said to her, talking like one who had been circumcised three or four times before. "Handle the herbs and you won't feel the knife."

But nothing could have prepared Chelimo for the searing pain that went through her entire system as the concoction touched first her labia then her clitoris. She had never felt such pain in her entire life before. The searing sensation lasted several minutes during which she felt her body begin to go on fire. Soon she felt a new sensation, carrying her into numbness.

All the parents broke into celebration chants as each girl finished the herbal treatment bravely without crying. They all knew how important this ritual was- the coward would be ridiculed and returned to the river to repeat the whole process. And if the *cemerik* eventually passed the test after returning from the river, she would be the last in the queue to be circumcised.

Firmly lying on the ground and legs open, Chelimo felt her organs rise up as though saluting the rising sun whose first rays could just be detected over the mountain. The cold mountain air blew strong, sending the bigger forest trees in a gentle sway and the pines in a low quiet whistle. In the distance the dogs, back from a night of mating, were barking their triumph and pleasure. The early birds always found the dry season a little challenging- to get the worms you had to come out even earlier. Today they were quite early.

The two girls lay side by side, staring straight up, waiting for the *mutik* but Chemtai managed to stretch a hand to touch her best friend in encouragement. Chelimo was glad she had Chemtai by her side.

When the girls settled and their genitalia mingled with herbal concoction, the *mutik* made her way, slowly through the huge crowd, knives up, to the front, attracting a huge applause. Yapcherop was a celebrity as she had handled many operations over the decades gone by. Everyone rubbed their hands in anticipation in an atmosphere charged with tension. The knives were laid on a small wooden table. A keen eye could see that unlike the blade for male circumcision which was straight, these ones were curved, like proper harvest knives, very much like a scythe or scoop. More importantly, they looked as sharp as could be.

Yapcherop took no more than 30 seconds with each girl expertly applying *rotwet* to her charges. The *mutik* assisting her blew the whistle after each successful harvest, attracting ululations as the people celebrated the harvest of *rotwet.*

The *mutik* washed her hands after each operation.

*****

As the car wafted along the smooth tarmac, Chelimo wondered whether those after her daughter would even wash their hands in preparation. She could visualise the ugly dirty hands vying for her daughter's... She did not even want to think about it.

*****

Chemtai did not flinch one bit and when *rotwet* had duly harvested what belonged to her, it turned out that she was not afraid to cross the red line a second time, going into even deeper territory. It must have been something the old woman had said before, about respecting elders, that riled Chemtai.

"Sip!" Chemtai cursed - rather than declared. "I'm Chemtai daughter of the Kapsumbata clan; and don't you ever talk to me like that again stupid woman. Nobody talks to Chemtai like that."

Everybody was taken aback they didn't know what to think. Fortunately there was just one more *cemerik*. Yapcherop was taken aback too but moved on to the last person, Chelimo.

Chelimo's mind was as numb as her body but she felt another sharp pain go through her system as the curved knife expertly scooped out her clitoris and everything that surrounded it. She felt the knife slicing off her labia in a quick but casual manner. She felt her body curve into a permanent gap. She did not flinch.

She stared up and swore by her clan.

"Sip! I'm a daughter of the Kapsulel clan!"

Yapcherop was relieved that the last charge had not provided any more drama. In all her years as a surgeon she had never been insulted and she was not even sure of how to react. The rules stipulated that girls had to apologize to elders for any insults lest a curse struck them and the wound refused to heal. The other punishment was that the genitalia would return as though they had never been cut off. That would mean that the girl would have to undergo the whole process again. Yapcherop simply rolled up her gear. Her work was done. She would only have to periodically check on the progress of the healing process.

The final whistle was blown announcing that it was all over, causing an eruption of rapturous celebration.

Bed sheets were passed around to cover the girls. Their mothers began dancing, praising the candidates for their bravery. The mothers to the members of the *Bunda* were the chief guests at the ceremony. They had their own special drinks and their own hut.

More herbs were squeezed onto the wounds of every girl to mark the beginning of the healing process.

Local brew too was sprinkled on the fresh wounds. Healing of genital wounds usually took two weeks maximum. There could be slight variations here and there of course, but give or take, a few days.

After the celebrations, the girls were led to a confined place where privacy was guaranteed. They were there together for a while. It was a shelter that had been erected up a hill. There were no roads on the small hill and no strangers asking impossible and unreasonable questions. Nobody else had an excuse to be there except the girls and those attending to them.

The girls were told that over the years it had been proved that some girls healed faster and were up and about in barely one week; the slow healers would need two weeks or sometimes, a little more. Nothing to be afraid of, they assured them.

Chelimo took three weeks to heal - if she did ever heal. Although the physical wounds made steady progress, those on her mind were still fresh. For her best friend Chemtai, the girl who slapped her mentor back and insulted the *mutik* – had not only failed to heal like the others, but she was in critical condition and they feared for her life. The matter sent a tremor through the community especially her *Bunda.*

The elders said that if it had never happened, it was only because nobody had ever had the temerity to slap one's mentor or insult a surgeon; it simply had been too much for the spirits and they had apparently had no choice but to inflict punishment. But some women quietly whispered that it had happened many times before and that many girls had died from their wounds but it was not wise or safe to talk about it. Everything ugly about circumcision had been hushed up over the years.

The *rikset* which was the final pass-out ceremony was scheduled to begin in the evening, a few weeks after the circumcision and it was expected to last through the entire night till morning. Local brew was prepared and lots of food and meat cooked. The girls were taken to Sipi Falls on the side that was shielded by numerous trees and banana plantations and taken through the final initiation rites. On another day this ceremony could have been taken to a banana plantation or a forested hilltop; but most people preferred a river. Every one of the 20 girls of the *Bunda* showed up- except Chemtai. They were well aware that shying away from the final ceremony amounted to remaining a girl even though one had been circumcised. Absconding from the final ritual also meant that one would not even be allowed to escort girls to the river during subsequent circumcision years or to attend the training of the girls at any stage.

Amidst the eating and drinking of clansmen and women, the girls were taken through the secrets of the river; they were told everything about circumcision so that they too could pass it on to their daughters and granddaughters. It was at this point that each of them was taken to meet the sacred leopard so that it could sink its teeth into their arms. The four marks showing where the four canine teeth of the leopard had hit would be their eternal identity, showing that they had been initiated into womanhood to the very end of the ritual. Nobody could forge the mark of the leopard; somebody had tried it and got embarrassed because the marks did not resemble those made by the leopard.

The merrymaking lasted all night. The girls were declared adults, ready to face the world; full women. More importantly, they had a new family. If you were circumcised at the same time and point with some other girl, she was your "*mbasuben*"; her children were your children. But in some cases those who were circumcised within three seasons of each other were still considered to belong to the same *Bunda*.

After circumcision, those girls who wanted to marry could do so; they were told. Chelimo thought this was a completely superfluous statement - why would one kiss *rotwet* for no other reason than to be a good wife to somebody's son? She kept her counsel but briefly entertained the hypothesis that Chemtai would be happy to float the question had she been around.

Chelimo's thoughts wandered again - as they almost always did - to the condition of her friend. She made a mental note to check on Chemtai before reaching home but her thoughts were interrupted by the sound of commotion that rose well above the general rumpus and brouhaha from the merrymakers. A few of the girls attempted to dash out to see what was happening but they were ordered back into their places by the mentors; under no circumstances were they allowed or supposed to move out.

It turned out a couple of uninvited guests had wanted to gatecrash the *rikset* but were intercepted by the bouncers at the entrance. The bouncers had asked them a couple of questions which they could not answer. For such occasions, there were passwords to entry. The gate crashers had stammered through their answers as they gambled here and there. The bouncers had needed no further invitation to pounce on the unfortunate lasses. They were beaten and chased like dogs.

It was at the *risket* that Chelimo started speaking to Esther, one of the girls in her *Bunda.* Esther was from the Kabokir clan. As they talked, Chelimo discovered that Esther was much older than any of the girls in this Bunda. Esther confessed to Chelimo that she was already married.

"How come you are here then?" Chelimo asked.

That made Esther open up. She was a social worker who hailed from Benet Sub- County and had been married to a progressive man from the Kapsumbata clan. She worked at the district headquarters of Kapchorwa but life had been difficult for her as an uncircumcised woman. She had enjoyed no respect from her husband and had been the subject of sheer contempt from her in-laws who Esther said that they never wanted their son to marry a coward. The societal sanctions had been too much to bear. Even at the well she was not allowed to get water until those who had been bitten by the leopard were done.

She was not allowed to talk in a public place – whether to address a gathering or make a contribution. She had not been able to enjoy a drink with grown-ups or join any progressive group. More importantly, she had intentions to contest for political office, but there was no way anybody would listen to a woman who did not know the secrets of the river.

Another friendship had begun.

"But what exactly made you miss being circumcised at the time when you should have?" Chelimo asked her.

Esther had sighed and told her young, new found friend, about her past.

Chelimo also told Esther about her teacher's story. Nobody ever came to know where teacher Jane Cheptoyek actually spent her childhood days. Versions of her story were only whispered here and there by people who said that the daughter of *Pondet* Kipsang - who everybody agreed was lovely to behold - had been educated in Kampala. When she came to Tegeres as a teacher, not much was known about her or where she had been. But Cheptoyek, whose name suggested her mother had given birth to her while she was away on a visit, never said much. She was a quiet soul who was at peace with herself and with everyone else around her and was used to having male flies abuzz about her. So she didn't do anything to thwart or accept the attentions of the suitors. She talked to them like she did anyone else with neither fear no favour.

It was a year down the road, after the initial purring about her beauty had worn off that a female colleague, Miss Alinyo, in an unguarded moment in the staffroom, asked her if she had kept in touch with the members of her *Bunda*, the group of girls whom she'd been circumcised with. There were eight age-sets - *Bunutek* - among the Sabiny: the Nyongi, the Somonion, the Mbatwa, the Muchungu, Korongoro, Kwoymet, Mnyikew and Kaplwalach. The age-set or *Bunda* one belonged to was evidence of one's circumcision and it was a strong and recognized sisterhood. You could not hold a function without the members of the *Bunda*. The offence was considered aggravated if it was a circumcision ceremony: there was a risk the *Bunda* would come and demand a heavy fine, which usually meant picking anything they fancied in your compound. They could slaughter your favourite bull and roast it at leisure, without any problem.

The *Bunda* of the girls were not as close-knit because girls, with time, got married and left their villages for places far off. But they nevertheless kept in close contact as sisters. Each of them carried four marks on the inside of their left arm-on the other side of the elbow. That was the spot where Malilyo the legendary leopard was believed to sink his teeth during the rikset, the special post-circumcision ritual that marked the final initiation into adulthood. As Miss Cheptoyek always wore long sleeved clothes, it had never been obvious whether or not she had ever met Malilyo.

Even with all her composure, Miss Cheptoyet was taken by surprise with her friend's question and after an initial stammer, confessed to her colleague that she didn't belong to any *Bunda.* It was unusual for a young woman not to belong to any *Bunda*, because it was unusual for a grown woman no to have been circumcised. Miss Alinyo who had never stopped extolling the beauty of becoming a woman and whose stories of bravado in the face of the knife and blood never knew any ending, (each story usually more elaborate than the previous one) had been even more surprised by her victim and soon told everyone that cared to listen that Cheptoyek had never made friends with Malilyo the leopard. As expected, Miss Alinyo took great liberty with the facts, embellishing her tale more each time she managed to pin down a person she could spin her yarn to.

It was at the next parents meeting that *Pondet* Kiprop, a man known for his oratorical skills and for speaking his mind, broached the matter. The substantive agenda of the meeting had been exhausted and the chairman was in fact feeling happy that not only had the parents kept time in reporting; they had also been fully cooperative, endorsed the new proposals for extra classrooms and an extra pay for the teachers. The meeting was going to end well ahead of schedule. His eyes went down to the bottom of the agenda to the item marked "Any Other Business, AOB." He was certain there would not be much here as everyone seemed eager to end the meeting and go to the very last item-which was never listed on the agenda but which to some, remained the most important: refreshments.

Just then he spotted the hand of *Pondet* Kiprop raised rather casually, almost reluctantly.

"I'll allow *Mokoryondet* Kiprop to raise any other business very briefly before we go for refreshments," said the chairman, a keen eye on the waitresses who were ferrying trays of eats and crates of drinks. It was enough to refer to Kiprop as *Pondet* (the title used to refer to or address distinguished elderly men), but such was Kiprop's stature that only *Mokoryondet* would do.

Kiprop got up in a relaxed manner and began to speak. He belonged to the Kwoymet *Bunda* (a fact he always pointed out every time he introduced himself at a public event) and had no fear of anybody or anything.

"A man that is too modest will go hungry," he began. Everyone laughed.

"Speak! Speak people are hungry," said the chairman, looking at his watch and then at the snacksS.

"What I'm saying Mr. Chairman is that let's not put a table on the issues; it is time to put issues on the table."

He paused for effect, took a suspicious look around and then proceeded.

"Mr. Chairman I seek to know whether it is in order for a teacher to train our children – especially the girl-children, when she herself has been as cowardly as the eye; she has never proved herself a woman."

In the uproar that followed – everybody talked at the same time, discussing the issue at the top of their voices until the chairman banged the table. The story of Miss Cheptoyek was not new; but nobody had had the boldness to make it an issue.

"So what do you expect the poor girl to do?" someone asked.

"It is not wisdom when the egg fights a cock," replied *Mokoryondet* without hesitation. "She can choose to become a woman, or return by the same way she came."

The applause that followed told the chairman there was no need to vote on the matter.

It was the following week when reality hit Cheptoyek hard. Her pupils refused to enter class; they stayed under the mango tree on the far side of the school compound. When she urged them in, they timidly explained what they had been instructed to do and not to do. Not going into a class being taught by "a girl", moreover "a coward", was part of what they were not supposed to do.

All the children started avoiding her. It was only her favourite pupil – Chelimo who insisted on interacting with her teacher without any reproach. The headmaster did not intervene. The fellow teachers kept to themselves in the staffroom or in their classrooms. From then on, Miss Cheptoyek could do nothing right. She was like a stepchild; accused of wasting water when she washed her hands and called dirty and scolded when she didn't wash.

“A coward at 35 is a coward forever,” the parents told their children.

Uncircumcised women were not allowed to prepare food. They could not climb into the granary because it was believed that if they did, they would bring bad luck to the family, possibly spoiling the next harvest. In the meetings of women they were not allowed to give opinions. Neither were they allowed to step into the kraal even if it was to get cow dung to use in smearing the house with. It was said that the cows would die or fail to produce milk or to bear more offsprings. Another very disturbing fact was that when an uncircumcised woman died, their bodies could not be passed through the main entrance of the house – instead, the family would dig an exit in the behind wall specifically for that purpose.

Life was tough when you were uncircumcised and death was tough when you died uncircumcised. But this was the first time the no-teaching dimension was being introduced. It had no precedent, but the community agreed with it; it was well in line with tradition handed down over the generations. It was the headmaster who had a complex problem on his hands: although he could not allow Cheptoyek to teach, pursuant of the resolution of the parents, he had no legal ground or authority to terminate her services as she was a government employee. So even though she received her salary every month, she was denied the joy and fulfilment that came with practicing one’s profession.

Cheptoyek always walked home head low, heart heavy and dreary. Some said that even though people did not become left-handed in old age, the beautiful teacher had almost developed a hunchback. It was the following August a few months after the incident – that the bubble burst.

On her way home from school one evening, Miss Cheptoyek was grabbed by a gang of strong young men and delivered to a group of elderly women who were waiting at the town square as everyone joined in a rather gay chant – a well-known *Chekwoyet*, but this time sang in a rather militant manner; clearly an angry army going to war. A just war, to right a wrong against the people.

Kachenam chito ...... ooooohhh!!! x 4 (We've finally caught the long-elusive person....ooooohhh!!).

Kachenam chito...... aaaaaaah!!! (We've finally caught the long-elusive person.....aaaaaaah!!).

Yakte posodebich...........ooooooooooooooh!! x 4 (You pay the debt that you owe the people...oooooohh!.

Yakte posodebich...........aaaaaaaaaaaaaaah!! (You pay the debt that you owe the people....aaaaaaaaaaahh!!).

She was taken to the town square where four poles had been erected. The town square was the place reserved for the circumcision of cowards, so as to cleanse the land. They tied her limbs to each of the poles and the *mutik* who had been reserved beforehand appeared from nowhere and set to work with her *rotwet*. The entire public cheered as the culprit was brought to justice. *Pondet* Kipsang was caught in between supporting his daughter's free spirit and staying loyal to the traditions of his forefathers.

Although the community had been united in ostracizing her, they were united in welcoming the village teacher into womanhood, merrily joining in the song-singing.

It was clear warning that defaulters would by no means escape. For Cheptoyek, the humiliation was more than she could bear. She simply disappeared.

"Went the same way she came… just like that," some people said, with a shrug of the shoulder. "At least she went a woman," others said.

The forceful circumcision of Miss Cheptoyek was talked about around the community for a long time. Circumcision was only done in the even years and the season officially closed on December 31st. But the surgeons had a right to look for cowards who had avoided the knife and bring them to order. That could be done any year, anytime.

The incident did send a tough message that there would be no tolerance for cowardice. The stigma of the shameful spectacle was so strong; even those who had entertained fear hastened to enlist for initiation the following season. Any reservation or misgivings about circumcision were shoved aside; all the girls realized they had no choice. The shame of forced circumcision was too much to even be contemplated.

Chelimo – who had been close to Miss Cheptoyek - had observed the transformation of a bright, elegant, inspirational teacher into one gloomy, dull and withdrawn woman. Her stoop stood out as if she had had it all her life. The forced circumcision and the shame and stigma that came with it hadn't helped matters. Chelimo had suffered with her mentor and was broken-hearted when she left. But she also realized that whatever misgivings she had about facing *rotwet* were misplaced; she had no options – nobody had an option in fact against the *rotwet*. They hastened to enlist for initiation the following season.

*****

A few days later, Chelimo was coming from the gardens when she saw two mentors walking together. A heavy downpour the night before had made the steep and slippery path even more treacherous, making the two old women watch their every step as they began the steep descent towards the town. Years of mountain climbing had taught her that no matter how difficult ascending a steep mountainside could be, it could never compare to the descent. She watched and listened to the old women as they moved slowly and in staccato style, with no particular rhythm to their walk because every step was calculated and often hesitant in relation to the ground.

Their conversation also came out in the same staccato manner, words often delayed as the old women paused to hold firmly onto the shrubs or the protruding rock, as they negotiated their way downhill. Chelimo noticed with sadness the satchels they carried and she knew what their mission was. These were the satchels which housed several versions of the knife of redemption. The same knives which had shed the blood of hundreds, or possibly thousands, of young girls as they initiated them into womanhood. Kapchorwa was never short of surgeons. There was roughly one surgeon within every 10 kilometre radius and so every *mutik* was not only in demand during season, she was also highly respected. The surgeons carried Kapchorwa's spirit. They carried the destiny of many a young woman in their hands - *wonset* was a delicate ritual where there was no room for mistakes; only the very experienced were allowed to do it. Their apprentices took years watching and learning- not to mention the rigorous instruction that took hours on end – before they were allowed to shed their first blood.

"So how are your women doing?" It quietly amused Chelimo to hear that after *wonset,* she and her *bunda* were now referred to as "women". Her childhood, her innocence were gone. She was now officially an adult.

"Well ... er... I think on the whole they are fine;" answered the other woman.

"You don't seem certain; is anything the matter?"

"Well, the other girl does not seem to be like the rest."

"Which one?"

"Chemtai, the daughter of Kulany. She has grown weaker over the last few days; we are not sure if she will make it at all. For her sake we delayed the *risket* by more than a week, until we couldn't push it any further. Now all the other girls have had their *rikset*." It dawned on Chelimo that the two women were talking about her *Bunda.* She was amused that she had not recognised the woman that had participated in the rituals of her *Bunda.* They are all the same, she hissed and spat.

"Ah! Chemtai who slapped her *makuryondent* and insulted the *mutik*? That's a sad story; it is long since we last had a thing like that. But you know that every circumcision year the spirits make their decisions and who are we to stop them? But how about the others; are they well?"

"The others are all progressing well. There should be no problem. Surgeon Yapcherop is a *mutik* with a good hand. It is rare for things to go wrong when she is in charge. I just don't understand what could have gone wrong. In fact, she has just been taken to the big hospital."

"You mean Kapchorwa Hospital?"

"Yes. Staff at Kapchorwa Hospital are used to treating circumcision complications and have done so over the years. But the case of Chemtai is bad; the Medical Superintendent (himself a consultant gynaecologist) came down to the examination room to see for himself.

"Did you go with the girl?"

"Yes."

"Next time you should never dare. You will be arrested."

"Of course I pretended I was Chemtai's grandmother. I never said I was a *mutik.* Now I fear, *mi kukuro poyik* - the ancestors beckon." The old woman narrated that the doctor took one look at the poor girl and started blinking to arrest tears just in time.

He'd demanded to know why the girl hadn't been brought in earlier, but got no response. Within seconds he had apparently already determined that nothing could be done to save the poor girl.

He had then pulled the old woman aside and told her the truth, only adding that he would however try and help her die with dignity.

Chelimo had at that point hurried past the two hobbling women and she went straight to hospital to find Chemtai. She arrived just in time to find her best friend being bundled off her bed and quickly wheeled out of the ward to avoid upsetting other patients. She was gone. Weeping bitterly, Chelimo followed the mortuary attendant until her friend's last stop for the time being - the cold room where, alongside other bodies, hers would be preserved till the relatives picked her up.

Chelimo faithfully stayed at the mortuary and accompanied her best friend every step of the way, till she was lowered into the grave. While everybody else threw in fists of earth as the priest went through the "dust to dust" motions, Chelimo threw in flower after flower, her vision blurred by tears that flowed freely like a waterfall in rainy season. She was inconsolable when the sound of spades scooping concrete and dumping it on the iron sheets and iron bars that covered the coffin filled the air. She had been brave enough when she faced *rotwet* at the river, which was supposed to be the acme of pain. But there was pain far greater; for while *rotwet* had sliced off her genitalia then; this time *rotwet* had pierced her right through the heart. She saw no reason why Chemtai had to go. It was like a lamp had been blown out; and from then on, few things made Chelimo smile. Slowly, almost imperceptibly, she developed into a sad-faced young lady.

Chemtai, had become another circumcision statistic. Yet Chelimo knew, the next circumcision time, the girls would be told; no death had ever occurred from circumcision in this land. They would agree. Silence would prevail.

"*Mi kukuro poyik....*" The words of the old mutik echoed endlessly in Chelimo's head from that day onward.

*****

Chelimo heard the driver hoot. Body and mind, she was back in the midst of a crisis, seeking her daughter.

"Where are we?" she asked the driver.

"We are about to reach Mbale. We still have a long way to Kapchorwa."

"Hmm. As if I don't know it," she grumbled then cupped her chin in her right palm.

"My baby, where are you? May the good Lord protect you from the evil kidnappers. God, how I wish I knew where and how she is! Daisy dear, darling, where are you?" she despaired.

Chapter Five

Daisy too was thinking about her mother. She found herself calling her, mumbling the word mummy all the time, asking herself why she was being held captive on a day her mother was away when she had no help at all and why her mother had to be away that very day.

She was too scared to even cry. After grabbing her as she entered the small gate to her home, she had screamed and tried to extricate herself from the men but they laughed at her and told her to shut up as they gagged her.

"You don't want to die, or do you?"

She shook her head in response.

"Then you must shut up."

After grabbing her, they had lifted her and put her back into the car and strapped her with a seat belt. The car then shot off at such a high speed that Daisy knew anytime it would crash into something. The man who sat next to her put his hand in his jacket pocket and fished out a piece of cloth before addressing her.

"Young girl, we are not going to harm you at all. Do you understand?"

"And you can choose how you want to be treated - with care if you cooperate or without care if you do not cooperate. It's all up to you," one of the men growled.

"We are taking you to a place where what will be done to you will be for your sake, to secure your future so that you become a true girl of the tribe and later, a proper Sabiny woman. Therefore, do not be afraid. We are not killers, we are not cruel. We are your best friends. We are only going to cover your mouth because we do not want you screaming all over the place. Screaming will make you develop a headache. And it will not be safe for all of us. But soon we shall remove the cloth after you have settled down," he paused. "Do you understand?" he continued in a calm voice.

She looked at him, her eyes darting left and right, confused. Terrified.

"I want my mother," she said.

"You will soon see your mother. And she will be very happy with the new you," he assured her.

"If you knew she would be happy, why did you take me without her? Why did you have to wait when she was away? Why did you have to bring me by force?"

The men turned and looked at each other.

"Here, you need a drink,," the one with the cloth said to her, handing her a water bottle whose contents looked and smelt like orange juice.

She looked at the bottle as if it was snake venom.

"The juice is safe. Like I told you, we are not going to harm you. The journey is long and you need something in your stomach." She only stared at him without raising her hand to receive the juice. He shrugged in resignation and proceeded to tie the cloth over her mouth. She did not struggle because she realized that it would be futile to try and fight off these bulky men. The car abruptly turned around and drove in the opposite direction. It made many turns and sped up a hill eventually entering a wide gate. As soon as it stopped, the men quickly lifted

Daisy out and took her to a black car and strapped her with a seat belt and the car took off. She realized that it was the same kind of car in which they had taken her uncle when he died. Those cars from funeral homes. Her heart gave way to a fear beyond description. There were many road blocks on the way, and she prayed to God that they would be stopped but the black ambulance-like car was simply waved through each roadblock as if in connivance. . After several hours of silence, Daisy fell asleep. She was woken up by a loud phone conversation.

"Are you ready? We are about to arrive. Aaah? What do you mean? We don't want any delays. Remember?" The men in the vehicle all looked startled. The man speaking pressed a button on the phone and the voice from the other side flooded the car. They all listened in.

"That was just a small hitch but it was sorted."

"The question is simple. Are you ready?"

"Yes we are. I already said we are more than ready."

"Same spot we agreed on?"

"Same spot, yes. Same vehicle. A Honda CRV. Everything is in place."

The exchange took place at Sironko in the dead of the night. As soon as the little entourage entered a plain looking Honda CRV, they sped off into the mountains, slowly navigating the steep road. As the cocks of Kapchorwa competed to announce the coming of yet another day, Fabio rolled the car gently, quietly and expertly into a deserted wooded area in Kapsulel village, Kwoti sub-county. The little entourage then began a steep climb up the mountain, Adeni leading the way, Fabio carrying the cargo, the object of their attention. They only rested when they entered a small, non-descript compound about three kilometres up the mountain, at the home of Emily Cherotich, an old widow. Cherotich, whose name means 'born as the cows returned from the pasture' lived mostly alone, with the exception of the odd gardener who came to help her from time to time.

The home had been chosen for largely strategic reasons. It was right on the edge of a dangerous precipice overlooking the little town of Kapchorwa. It was about three kilometres from the town, but it enjoyed a vantage view of everything that happened in the town. While standing in the town, it was almost impossible to notice the four or five little huts up the mountain, the vice versa had the opposite effect; anybody perched on the little homestead could see everything happening in the town. Besides, it was impossible to approach the home without being seen, not to mention the difficult treacherous climb. There were no idle passers-by to notice this or that; it was just the right place to stash away secret cargo and to carry out their business. The only intruders feared to be in this area were largely monkey hunters, looking to get monkey tails that would be used in the circumcision dances. There was one more strategic reason; Cherotich had been thrown out of job as a house-help by the minister in the earlier years when she could not cope with the demands of a house with a small child. The reason the Minister had insisted on keeping Cherotich was because she had children of her own and so the assumption was that she would be able to look after a child. That was not the case though. The Minister had tolerated her until on several occasions the baby cried and lost its voice and Cherotich would just look on like it was no problem at all. When one day the Minister told Cherotich that she did not want to find her daughter crying again, Cherotich had the audacity to tell her that all children cry. "Your child is not special."

"All I have asked is to ensure the child does not cry to the point of losing her voice.

"But madam all children cry. What do I do when I have to do housework and also attend to the child?"

The following day, the Minister told Cherotich to pack her belongings and leave.

"But Madam..."

"You will return when the baby is of age and able to look after herself."

"But..."

"I will give you a call as soon as we need you again."

The Minister gave her an equivalent of three month's salary and transport money to travel to the village by bus. She also gave her some clothes, bags and shoes. But Cherotich had still not wanted to leave, claiming that the Minister was being unfair.

"I have said that I will call you," the Minister had insisted.

Cherotich went home and waited in vain for the call. The rancour was so deep that Cherotich had never forgiven her. She had carefully nursed the grudge which was made worse by the fact that the Minister had not attended Cherotich's husband's funeral. Adeni's research had revealed all that and he was certain that clearly, Cherotich would not have to be sworn to secrecy. She would be happy to carry out her own revenge on the Minister and her snobbish household. Secrecy was further sealed by the big honorarium. He was certain that there was no way Cherotich could have made that kind of money as a maid in the Minister's kitchen, even if she had stayed until she was 90. Even though Cherotich was of the Kapsulel clan-like the Minister - Adeni was confident that the vendetta and the sheer value of the prize she stood to gain would keep Cherotich contented and most importantly, quiet.

In the compound stood four huts. Daisy was placed in the biggest hut. Adeni came close to her and reminded her to cooperate.

"This will be very simple, child if you cooperate. Do not do anything you are not told to do. Follow instructions to the dot. If you don't, we shall have no choice but to do what we all don't want." Daisy simply stared at the red-eyed man. She now knew she was completely at their mercy. She knew her mother would never find her in this deserted place. She knew she had only herself to depend on.

She was shown her bed just beside the old woman's bed. She would be helped with everything including bathing and visiting the toilet. Under no circumstances was she supposed to be on her own.

"I want to go back home," Daisy attempted.

"You will."

"When?"

"When our task is done. We shall let you know."

"I want to speak to my mother."

"No, you can't. We are sorry. From now on until you leave this place, she will be your mother," Adeni said, pointing at the old woman who had up to now been silent, her toothless mouth twitching up and down in a dangerous sneer. She stood with two other women who looked slightly younger than her.

The hut was not small inside. The outside appearance was deceptive. It was neat inside and the walls painted with colourful patterns.

"Sit down here child" the old woman wearing the green and black long dress invited Daisy. Daisy complied.

"I am the doctor who is going to set you free."Daisy felt a temporary twitch of happiness.

"Set me free? Oh grandma. Please set me free now so that I go back to my mother. Please," she pleaded.

The old woman shook her head.

"Tut, tut child," she mumbled. "You will soon go back to your mother. The freedom we are talking about is different. It is better than the one you are talking about.

Child, now you are like a prisoner in your own body. We shall set you free from some parts of your body which are stopping you from becoming a full woman of the Sabiny tribe. So child," she continued gently tapping on Daisy's stooped shoulders, "when we finish setting you free, you will go back to your mother. You will go back very, very happy, like a bird in the air." The old woman smiled as she led her to a mat spread on the floor. Daisy resisted. She turned to the door but the old woman stepped in front of her.

"Remember what your friend said? You must cooperate."

Daisy was disgusted. How could the old woman refer to her captor as a friend?

"He is not my friend and let me go!" She shouted. Before she could do anything, the men, her captors, materialised at the door. Daisy slumped down on the mat. Any hope of being set free evaporated. The women who she thought would set her free were part of the gang. She resigned herself to whatever fate awaited her.

Chapter Six

Chelimo sighed as her mind slowly got consumed with the past.... Her meeting with Dane, their love and courtship and subsequent marriage....the children....And now...

Chelimo met Dane at a bachelor's party. Her childhood friend Fiona was set to wed Mako whom she had been dating for quite some time. Bachelor's parties were in vogue and both the brides-to-be friends and relatives and the groom-to-be friends and relatives, all thronged these parties. It was a chance to celebrate the good fortune of the groom-to-be, but also a good opportunity to catch up with lost friends and make new ones. Chelimo who was sharing her apartment with Fiona prepared too for the party.

Her partner was a tall, strongly built young man of about twenty eight years; a great dancer who made no secret of his liking for her. Chelimo was therefore not surprised when he called her up three days after the party asking to meet her at Serena Hotel "just for a cup of coffee" he assured her.

*****

"Anyone called Chelimo can only hail from Kapchorwa," he said after they had placed their orders with the waitress.

Chelimo smiled in acknowledgment.

"And...What's the other name? You must be Chelimo something?" he probed.

"Tezira. But most people call me Tez. And what name accompanies Dane?"

"Twino. That is in short. The entire name is too long."

"What's the entire name?"

"It is Twinobusingye."

"How many letters?"

"That's not all. The full name is Twinobusingye Omuri Ruhanga."

"And what does that mean? I know all your names from that part of the country have meanings."

"But so are many of yours."

"Yes but not all. Anyway, mine means we have peace in the Lord. Many of our names are sentences," he laughed. Chelimo joined in the laughter.

"That's an understatement. Some are mini paragraphs!" She exclaimed and again they laughed.

"You are from the great Sabiny tribe of Kapchorwa?" he asked. "The country of the beautiful Sabiny women."

She held her breath, trying to trace signs of pretence or cynicism on his face as he mentioned the Sabiny women. But his face was relaxed and she could read adoration instead.

"You are right, Dane Twino. And I can straightaway tell that you are from western Uganda, from Kigezi."

"You are right but why Kigezi? This name can be found anywhere in Western Uganda."

"And your energetic build?"

"Ah well... that too can be from any part of the country," he said rubbing his muscular arms and tapping his left foot. Then, as an afterthought, he bent forward and said, "So, my dear newly-found Sabiny lady, I have to find a name for you."

"Why? I told you my name."

"Well well...I can't keep on calling you Chelimo. It sounds kind of formal, if you see what I mean. And Tezira...Tez...well... I am sorry, but I had a grandmother called Tezira. Loved her so much. But I associate the name with some...err...like elderly people," he coughed teasingly but also apologetically. "You know names like Tabitha. . . they fall into that category."

Chelimo laughed.

"Really Dane, that's kind of old fashioned thinking."

"No offence meant. But anyway, can I call you Cheli?"

Again she laughed.

"Well that's the first I am hearing it and it sounds kinda nice. Reminds me of cherries."

They both laughed.

Chelimo knew about the folks from the other end of the country. Bakiga men were usually tall and muscular; handsome in a rugged manner, the men with a knack for telling it like it is. Kigezi was a beautiful hilly country usually referred to as the Switzerland of Uganda. The mainstay of the people was agriculture and pictures of their terraced hillsides were a permanent engraving into the mind of every student of geography.

"Incidentally, what does your name mean?" Dane asked.

"I was born when the cows were coming home from the field," she replied.

"That's beautiful; brings to mind a tranquil atmosphere...romantic and divine," he beamed. Chelimo smiled. She was beginning to like this chap.

"Where do you work?" she asked.

"At the Ministry of Finance. And you?"

"Also a civil servant. I am with the Ministry of Energy."

"Ah!"

"What?" Chelimo frowned slightly.

"Nothing," he said as he poured her another coffee.

*****

After that they met almost every evening. They started going to the health club, playing badminton together and at the end of it all, they would join the scrabble group and enjoy the game until the closing time of ten o'clock. At the end of three months, they had become inseparable friends and one night after a game of scrabble as Dane gave Chelimo a lift to her place, he popped the question. To his consternation, she looked dismayed.

"Cheli, what's the matter? I thought the feeling of love between us is mutual. Or is it not? Look Cheli, we are both ripe for marriage. Our people say; *enyamwonyo kwekura eribwa.*"

"What does that mean?"

"When a bunch of banana becomes mature, it is harvested, cooked and eaten. Similarly when a girl matures, she gets to be courted and then married. Cheli, I love you. Please be my wife," he pleaded.

"Dane?"

"Yes?"

"You don't expect an answer now, do you? Besides, we have just met."

"I do expect an answer. And it's not true to say we've just met; it's a quarter of a year since we met! I can propose again while on my knees if that will show you my seriousness."

"That would be melodramatic Dane."

"Cheli?" he probed gently.

"Yes?" She sighed and looked at him. "Please give me time to think about it. It's kind of abrupt," she ended lamely.

"Really, darling? Abrupt? I thought we both saw it coming right from the word go."

"Saw what coming?"

"Our marriage. I felt the current go through both of us that very first night. Cheli, I am sure you also see that we belong together. Besides, I am a Mukiga. Bakiga do not go round in circles without saying what it is they want to say. We are not like those other people," he said as he dug his fingers into her ribs, causing her to laugh but only for a few seconds.

"Dane, its just that..."

"Just what Cheli?"

Silence.

"I need to know the truth. Do I have a...er...a competitor?"

"Why do you ask?" she laughed.

"Cheli, I know where you stand with me and it is right here on my left side. But it might not be the same with me. Do I stand here at your right side?" Dane said poking his hand into her right ribs. "I ask because I really want to know the truth."

"Okay." Chelimo took a deep breath before continuing. "Here is where you stand with me. Dane, I love you too. Incidentally, I have never had an affair before. You are my first and for now you are my only love. The love of my life. Believe you me Dane," she ended softly.

"Cheli my dear, I believe you and I really cannot imagine living without each other. It's not just your physical beauty though I mean, your looks really knock me down - your beautiful eyes full of warmth, your flawless chocolate skin and the whole package – God! You are a wonder. But there is something more in your soul – something else, something really beautiful. Please marry me."

"Dane, you heard what I said. Please give me time."

"Okay, name the time frame."

"Eeh!"

"Yes."

"Don't you trust me?"

"I do. One hundred percent. That's why I need the timeframe named.

"Okay. Two months?"

"Two months? Two months?" he groaned. "Cheli please don't torment me. Two months! Let's do it half-way: one month even though that is still too long. Agreed?"

"Okay," she said as she opened the car door.

He hugged her and planted a light kiss on her lips.

"Goodnight my dear and please let's continue to meet even during the agonizing one month. For me, it is going to be the longest month of my life."

She laughed lightly and quickly ran up to her apartment as Dane studied the Calendar on his cell-phone.

They continued to meet and the more they met, the more Chelimo loved him. He was everything she had always looked for in a husband to be. But she did not know how to tell him about the well-kept secrets of the river. May be she should just run away from the country, get a job in one of the neighbouring countries and give Dane space to get himself a wife who would live up to his expectations.

One night, after she returned from a date with him, she sat on her bed and held her head in thought about their relationship. She wondered whether to tell him or not to tell him. Maybe he would leave her after getting to know the truth. She was engulfed by all these thoughts when the light on her cell phone indicated an incoming call. It was Dane.

"Cheli," he started.

"Yes my love." She could smell anxiety all over his voice. She was happy that he too was thinking about her just at the same time.

"Maybe we are soul-mates," she blurted out without thinking.

"I agree."

"You won't even ask why I say so?"

"No. Because I have known that since we met. I am surprised you just got to know. But don't make me forget the reason I called."

"I am sorry. Please shoot."

"Cheli. Something is bothering you. I could tell but I did not want to ruin our evening and that's why I did not ask this evening when we were together.

"You could tell?"

"Yes, of course. Tell me, is what is bothering you the fact we that we come from different tribes?" he asked.

"Dane, I am even surprised that you proposed to me since you don't seem to think so highly of me! At this point in time and given my character and education, do you really think that would bother me? If we were to get married, I would be marrying you not your tribe!"

"Sorry dear. Take it that I never even asked the stupid question."

Chelimo laughed lightly and switched off the phone. On second thoughts she switched it on again. Dane called immediately before she put the phone down.

"Yes Dane?"

"You just switched off."

"I am sorry. Did you have other questions?"

"No. But I did not say goodnight. Neither did you."

"I am sorry again. It's because I was very busy doing something else when you called. So have a lovely night."

"Goodnight love and lets talk tomorrow."

A few days after Dane's proposal, Chelimo requested for the office double-cabin pick-up to take her to the village over the weekend.

"It's been quite a while since I last saw my parents. That is sinful. So I would like to go and check on them," she told the transport officer who agreed to provide her with the DC (Dangerous Car) as they referred to the car.

Chelimo bought two bright coloured bed covers for her parents and a pair of bed sheets each. They did not share a bed – each had their own: old people felt more comfortable each having their own bed, what with all sorts of pains and aches that come with old age, stiff joints and all that. They each needed their own space. She remembered that her mother had asked her to take her a nightdress the next time she went home. "Bring a big and long one. Not those small things of yours that look like you are putting on a banana leaf that has been hit by hailstones," her mother had advised. Chelimo had laughed and told her that she would not forget.

She bought her the longest nightdress she could find – one that threatened to sweep the floor. She also bought her father two pairs of pyjamas. She was aware that many men, even the modern ones, didn't care for pyjamas. Many of the modern ones just bought them for hospital – in case they fell sick and were hospitalised. They argued that underwear was good enough or even better, Adam's birthday suit. What the hell! They said that Uganda was too hot a country that no one needed extra heat on his body.

On Friday morning, Chelimo boarded the DC to Kapchorwa, her beloved home. There was always something therapeutic about being home. The journey, itself especially as she got nearer home, was always magical. She always preferred to travel the last fifty kilometers or so to her home in the evening as the sun bid the land good night. The beauty of the rolling hills never failed to amaze and gladden her heart. The road was now tarmacked, courtesy of the present government which had taken over the reigns of power in 1986. With the visionary leadership, the country had made steady progress in all sectors.

The tarmack road accentuated the beauty of the land as it weaved through the mountain. The beauty of her homeland always re-affirmed her thinking - that there was a higher being, a Creator, somewhere where nobody knew, may be somewhere up in what they called heaven, a magnificent force beyond anybody's imagination, an invisible hand that had curved out all those wonders of nature.

The DC under the experienced hand of the driver smoothly sailed on the tarmac and soon they were near the spot that always made Chelimo hold her breath as she watched everything as if for the first time. She told the driver to pull the DC to the roadside overlooking the falls and park. She got out of the car and started walking.

From a corner and entering another hill, the wonder of the Sipi Falls suddenly hit the serene green of the hills and valleys. It was a sudden flash of silken water gushing down, cascading under the afternoon sun, an invitation to move closer. Chelimo once again reflected upon God's greatness. From 400 meters above, the water pours majestically over the rocks forming twin streams. It passes through and over rocks stretched on the ground and forms a series of rapids that continue into the distance, disappearing somewhere under the main road to Mbale. On the right hand side of the twin streams, a huge banana plantation descends from the very top of the falls down to the bottom where the river meets the main road, lush green plants, beautiful and majestic to behold. To the left a blend of trees and grass descends and forms a little wooded area that both local and foreign tourists always walk through.

Chelimo crossed a little wooden bridge – several planks of wood, some long, others shorter, plastered across. She then began a steep climb up the banana plantation. By the time she got to turn down she was sweating and panting. She then began a slow slippery climb down, right, reaching where the water from a small stream poured from the rocks. She found a couple – young and white – bathing in what was a beautiful natural shower. They simply stood at the base of the cliff and the water poured on them as they played like little children. All one needed was soap and sponge… and towel may be, but the hot sun could be towel enough when the sun was high in the sky if one could wait a minute or two. She realized that the water, spraying and splashing freely had drenched her completely, but she didn't mind; in fact it was a pleasurable feeling.

Chelimo climbed down towards the bowl-like base where the river poured its white waters over the cliff. She stood near the splashing water. Within a few minutes, her clothes were wet. She was sprayed by the wishy-washy water from the splash effect on the rocks below. She closed her eyes and felt the water continue to touch her. It was a magical feeling.

Below the rocks, ten metres inward was a cave at whose entrance one could stand directly below the falls. It was a glorious and majestic sight which made her make up her mind to slap anyone who dared say that God did not exist. This part of the falls was Simba falls, named after the son of former Sipi River Lodge proprietor, Simba Rotich. Here the water fell on mighty rocks, making a huge roaring sound that reminded her of The Book of Revelation which says that the voice of the Lord roars like the sound of many waters.

She felt like taking a shower but feared to go in directly lest the unthinkable happened. Instead, she knelt beside the falls and prayed earnestly to the Lord to give her life the natural right course to take like he did with rivers despite hills, valleys and ragged landscapes. By the time she finished praying, the sun was going behind the hills in front of her. She hurried back towards the waiting DC and its driver. She knew she had to make it to her home in the fastest time possible before it became dark. She was always teased by the steep and slippery slope leading to their house.

But there came the difficult part of her adventure. Climbing back to the road, clearly described the phrase; up-hill task. She cursed her shoes and wondered why she, a daughter of Kapchorwa had not had the presence of mind to bring sports shoes. She had to walk on all fours like a cat but without its agility. She looked down and was frozen by fear. It was a mistake. A big mistake, because she almost collapsed with trepidation. She had forgotten the cardinal rule of every climber – do not look down while still climbing. She removed her shoes and held each in each hand. She quickly focused her eyes ahead of her as she continued to edge forward.

She was relieved when she got to the top of the cliff where the falls actually began. At the top the river was clear and slower before beginning its half kilometer descent. Children played around without a care in the world. Women washed their clothes, taking advantage of free-flowing water. Life here was normal, with a simplicity that was both pleasurable and enviable in many ways. It was another world altogether. Nobody congratulated the climber for successfully getting to the top but they smiled back when she smiled at them and greeted them in Kupsabiny.

Chelimo felt this was very much like the journey of life – you struggle to reach the top after incredible difficulty, only to find people who have been up there all along and they see nothing special about it. You are congratulating yourself but for them it is perfectly normal. She looked at the many benches donated by the Rotary Club of Kapchorwa and felt a deep desire to sit down and relax for a little while but she knew she was struggling against time. She took a long draught on the bottle of water that she had carried with her, before continuing to where the double cabin awaited her.

They rode on and as dusk begun to fall, Chelimo told the driver to take the next turning on the left. They were now on the rugged village road that led to her home. Chelimo was amazed at the fact that she never felt the bumps on this road because all the time she would be busy thinking of reaching her beloved home, of embracing her dear mother her head now a crown of pure white hair and of seeing her dear Papa. With most of his teeth gone, his cheeks were deep sunken as he always sucked them in maybe to fill the gap that the missing teeth had left. These thoughts always made Chelimo's eyes sink with a film of wetness brought by a mixture of joy tinged with an unexplained sadness.

The sound of the car had already gotten the old couple out of the house. There on the verandah, they all waited as the car slopped down. Chemaswet, Chelimo's older sister's son of four, held tightly on his grandmother's long dress, half scared, half anxious staring at the car and the people it carried. Chemaswet's mother had dropped out of school, got married and was just breeding babies.

"*Eyo*, Papa," Chelimo cried as she jumped out of the DC and rushed into first her mother's arms and then her father's. It was a happy re – union and Simba the dog who did not want to be left out of the action came from the backyard barking excitedly and then wagging his tail while whining in its welcome to Chelimo. He jumped up and down around her and Chelimo laughed touching and rubbing its head.

"Simba! Ever the same," she said as she lovingly stroked his back. They entered the modest but neat house. With part of her first salary, Chelimo had refurbished her parent's house. Building in the same mud and wattle structure and replacing the temporary materials with brick and cement. She roofed with the now fashionable versatile iron sheets. She was lucky the rural electrification programme had reached their village and now the energy saver bulbs lit the modest house. Her parents could never stop expressing their joy that they had managed to educate their girl and it had paid off in more ways than they ever thought. In fact when she went to secondary school, the men who had wanted to marry her had threatened the parents telling them that she would certainly return home pregnant before completing school. It was by faith that they had persisted and now they were reaping very pleasurable fruits, making villagers jealous.

Chelimo got busy giving out what she had brought for her parents and later making their beds in spite of her mother's protest that they could do it themselves and that Chelimo should rest after the long journey from Kampala City. Chelimo however could have none of it and remained busy participating in every evening chore. After supper, she still wanted to talk to them but it was time for bed. She understood because for most old people in most parts of the country, going to bed early was the norm.

Chelimo had made her bed in the bedroom she had occupied as a child. There was a strong bond with her and that bedroom – maybe every grown up felt that almost mystical connection with their childhood bedrooms. When she started work among the things she had bought was a medium sized bed. She jumped onto her bed and pulled the covers. Kapchorwa was always cold. Even during the hot season, it was not unusual to have cold nights. She closed her eyes and tried to sleep but sleep evaded her. A lot was going on in her mind.

After several turns and twists, she jumped out of bed and went straight to her parent's bedroom. They were both already snoring. Whereas her mother snored softly, her father's snoring was louder and rugged. Chelimo tiptoed to her mother's side of the bed and she tapped her softly on the shoulder.

"*Eyo* - Mama, I want you to come and sleep in my bed," Chelimo's whisper was like a gentle wind.

The old woman woke up quietly and without asking any question, she put on her slippers and followed her daughter to her bedroom. Chelimo had always known her to be like that. Dependable.

"Are you okay?" she asked the daughter as soon as they got into the bedroom.

"Yes *Eyo*. I am okay."

It was rare for Chelimo to refer to her Mother in Kupsabiny. Whenever she did, the mother knew she really needed her attention.

Chelimo laid back the covers and asked her mother to get into bed.

"It's a cold night as usual, *Eyo*. But these hills are always like that."

"Yes it is," her mother responded as she slipped in between the covers. Chelimo followed suit. She pulled the covers over both of them and her arm found its way around her mother's bosom. Interesting, the feel of the soft, wrinkled body next to hers gave Chelimo great comfort and a sense of security and peace. There were a few minutes of silence and then the old woman turned to her daughter.

"Child, you can now tell me about it. And you should never worry too much. There is always an end to every problem."

Chelimo did not have to tell her that a huge load was resting on her head. *Eyo* just knew and that is how it had always been. Chelimo told her the story of Dane, the Mukiga man, from Kigezi land and of how they had met, their friendship and eventual proposal and how Chelimo had said she wanted to tell him something before she could give him an answer. How she had asked him to give her one month to think about it. How two weeks were already gone by and she had no decision yet.

"So *Eyo*, I have come to seek your advice. Should I tell him about it?"

The old woman knew what the 'it' was.

The silence that followed was heavy.

"Do you feel in your heart that he is the man you want to spend all your life with? Is he the man you want to produce children with, cook for and look after? Is he the one you want to spend your nights with under the same blanket breathing his breath and him breathing yours?"

That summarized *Eyo*'s way of asking whether Chelimo loved Dane.

"Is he the one, my child?"

"He is, *Eyo*."

"Then tell him. He will either say he wants to marry you or he doesn't want to marry you."

For *Eyo*, it was that simple.

"Thank you *Eyo*. It will be as you say. On the fifteenth of August, I will tell him."

"Why the fifteenth?"

"That's what we agreed."

"I wish you luck my daughter."

"Thank you *Eyo*."

The old woman sighed again and in the darkness, tears of pity for her child quietly flowed. She turned and faced the wall again and let the tears run uncontrolled. She did not want her child to see them or to know that she was crying. She was always trying to shield her daughter from the cruelties of the world. But Chelimo knew that her mother was hurting. The bond between them was so strong that each always knew the feeling of the other.

Chelimo's embrace tightened a tiny wee bit as if to reassure her mother not to worry too much.

"*Eyo*, thank you," she whispered again.

Chelimo put her arm back onto her mother's bosom and they slept, each preoccupied with a shared fear.

But Chelimo slept for a short time and then woke up. She called her mother.

"*Eyo*?"

"Yes?"

"If circumcision causes insufferable pain, why has it gone on all these years? Why? Why? Tell me. Why?"

"You have asked me the same question before."

"Yes. And I am asking you again."

"You went to school. I did not. If you did not discover the answers when you left these hills and went to live out there, then maybe it's the same old answers that I will still give you."

"Why can't the women simply say no to all this!"

"You are shouting."

"I am sorry. But why *Eyo*. Why?"

"Child, we know too many things but we keep quiet about them. Sometimes it is better to live like that," she said. "Now, we must sleep. These questions will not return what was long taken away from us. They will simply torture us. I hope you will sleep."

Chelimo did not answer. She did not want to lie to her mother that she would sleep well. At the same time she did not want to worry her further. As her mother slipped into slumber land, Chelimo tried to comfort herself that at least she had gotten the answer to Dane's proposal from the most trustworthy person in her life.

Chapter Seven

Sunday morning, Chelimo boarded the DC back to the city, armed with the courage to tell Dane.

Days had quickly rolled into a month. August fifteenth was here. Dane had noted in his diary the date when Chelimo said she would give him an answer. This was the d-day. Fifteenth August was also the day of the Blessed Virgin Mary, according to the Christian Faith. In his part of the country, the months of June, July and part of August were the height of the dry season when most bushes even caught fire. However the fifteenth of August was considered miraculous by the Christian Community in that the heavens never disappointed. The much awaited rain would always pour forth, not in destructive torrents but good, smooth rain that would be smelling of the earth. People, especially women, would then wake up early the following morning carrying baskets of millet seed on their heads, heading to the already prepared gardens. The fifteenth of August was therefore, a divine miracle for Christians.

"Maybe this is prophetic," Dane said to himself. "I believe Cheli's answer coming on the same day, will be guided by the blessed virgin. She will say yes to my marriage proposal," he continued, half believing, half doubting.

It was exactly midnight when Chelimo's mobile phone rang. She usually switched off her phone at ten thirty after Dane's goodnight call but these past two weeks she left it on the whole night because her mother had told her that Papa was not feeling too well after her visit to the village. She therefore kept the phone on, in case her father developed some complications at night and they failed to reach her.

The phone woke her up from a nightmare where some monster with bared teeth and claws had been chasing her but when it was about to grip her, she grew wings and flew far, far away into the clouds and laughed down at it. She felt great like superman. Like those dreams she used to get when she was a child. She grabbed her phone and the first thought was that her papa's condition had worsened. In the panic, she pressed the 'off' button instead of 'ok'.

"Oh God what have I done?" She rebuked herself as she tried to call back but the phone rang again. Quickly she switched on the bed side lamp and looked at the number. It was Dane whom she had saved as "The one."

"Honestly darling! Do you, by any chance, have any idea what time of the night it is?" she asked with mock annoyance.

"Say, what time of the morning it is sweetheart. It is a few minutes past midnight and the date is fifteenth August in case you had forgotten," Dane said, sounding alert and fresh.

"Oh! God. Fine I remember it's the fifteenth of August but hadn't you slept?"

"Say that again."

"Did you have to wake me up at this time? For God's sake I thought we had a date after work this evening."

"Be honest with yourself. Did you expect me to be asleep?"

"Why not?"

"Say that again."

"What's wrong with your hearing tonight?"

"You are whispering baby."

"The reason we should not be talking at this ungodly hour."

"Oh, please. You know what I want Cheli. This has been the most agonizing month of my life and you are extending my torture! Have mercy on me," he begged.

"Honey, you sound desperate!" Chelimo teased.

"I am."

"I am sorry. I didn't mean to torture you."

"Thank you." There was silence. "And?" Dane was not about to give up.

"And let's meet and talk this evening, at your apartment."

Dane screeched with joy. All this time Chelimo had refused to meet him at his apartment except when she was in the company of her friend, Fiona. When Dane pressed her for a reason, she told him that it was because she was avoiding leading both of them into temptation.

"A temptation I would be happy to be led into," Dane had replied in a deliberate slow voice, winking.

"I knew I was right," Chelimo had replied, adding that Dane should stop pressing since it was never going to happen anyway until it was time if ever it was to be.

Now was the time.

"Okay. Six at my apartment then. Let me start fumigating the place right away."

Chelimo laughed.

"Fumigate at midnight? Do you have all sorts of vermin as your tenants then?"

"The creatures that inhabit a bachelor's hovel my dear! Roaches, the bugs, you name them. Anyway, I don't want to take chances. And those pesticides and insecticides or any cides are toxic, you know. Have to give them enough time to quit the house after spraying. Don't want to take the risk of getting my darling wife to pop a limbless tot or worse, into the world because of the damn chemicals."

Chelimo laughed and switched off the phone after she said goodnight. She tried to sleep. After all *Eyo* had told her not to worry.

In the morning Chelimo tried not to think about Dane. She somehow floated through the day apprehensive of the six O'clock appointment. When he called at five minutes to five to say he was down in the parking yard, waiting for her, her heart did a brief marathon.

"Okay. I am coming," she said feigning a calmness she was far from feeling. She picked her handbag and said, "See you tomorrow good people," to her officemates who were also picking their different items to go home. She headed for the staircase.

"The Lord is my shepherd I shall not want," she mentally kept repeating as she scouted for his car.

"Here sweetheart."

"Seen you already." Don't panic, her control button was telling her. Dane gave her a slight kiss on the lips as usual though this time, he let the tip of his tongue enter her mouth a little bit. To his pleasant surprise Chelimo held him tightly and when they separated, she smiled, making his hormones jump into turmoil.

"Is this a sign of good things to come?" he asked, smiling like a contented cat.

"Maybe," Chelimo replied, noncommittal. Dane eased the car out of the parking yard and on to the main street. The inside of the car was spotless clean and smelt like the night rose shrub that *Eyo* mother grew behind the house back home. Chelimo sniffed it in and closed her eyes.

Dane weaved through the maddening traffic jam of Kampala and turned into a cursing machine at every turn.

"Don't curse. The presence of so many cars is a sign of prosperity. That means many more people are getting into the money economy," said Chelimo.

"Well, there are attendant problems, though I think, it is the initial planners of the city who are to blame. Why didn't they plan for expansion?"

"Oh please. Do not start blaming Colonialists again. I don't like it when people blame Colonialist for all our ills. We must always look forward not backwards lest we be turned into pillars of salt like Lot's wife."

"Lot's wife?" Dane asked as he scratched his head.

Chelimo laughed.

"You mean you don't know the Bible?"

"Of course I know it." He sounded uncertain.

"Lot's wife had been accorded divine deliverance by the Lord as he destroyed the sinful cities of Sodom and Gomorrah but had warned her not to look back as fire and brimstone rained down from the heavens. But Lot's wife did...and she paid the price. So let's stop this blame game and move on," asserted Chelimo.

"Point taken Madam, point taken," he applauded with cynicism as he turned into the driveway of Forest Apartments where he resided. "Here we are honey," he said as he quickly jumped out of the car and opened the door for her. She laughed and realised that she was laughing a lot. She then knew it was the nervousness.

"Dane, what ceremony else? You remember the famous words in Shakespeare's Hamlet?"

"Vaguely. I was never one for reading that complicated Shakespearean English and stuff. By the time I would be through reading and deciphering ten sentences, I would develop such a throbbing headache! Is it worth it? I would ask myself."

"Interestingly for me, the pleasure lay precisely in that complicated, archaic English," Chelimo said.

"Cheli, stop involving yourself in things that make you crease your brows as you read. Read stuff that makes you laugh," Dane counselled as he opened the door to his apartment.

Chelimo was impressed by the neat décor of Dane's apartment. It was painted in orange colours which Chelimo thought was a trifle too bright, with flowered sofas of the same colour. It was a homely apartment. It had character and she told him so.

"Thank you," he said as he bowed in mock courtesy.

"May I kindly propose that you change your usual drink to a more exciting one?" he asked.

"You are allowed only one proposal a month. But yes, a glass of sweet white wine will do," she replied without hesitation.

"I am honoured. None of your usual drink you are sure? Tonight, none of your 'eat correct stuff Dane?"

"Now you are teasing. Look, I need it for the courage for what we are about to get into. And one day doesn't make meat rot, so our people say. One glass will not kill me."

Dane smiled as he inserted the CD in the Sony player. He had a good collection of jazz music and Chelimo found herself tapping her foot to the tune of the music. The lyrics filtered through music. Dane filled a long and thin wine glass with white wine and placed it on a small stool near Chelimo.

"They don't fill a wine glass like they fill a beer one," she teased.

"That's why I want you near me so you can teach me all those things," he said as he sat next to her and held her right hand. When she did not pull away like she always did, he extended his left hand as well.

"So, how will I drink my wine?"

"You will."

"You have made me a prisoner!"

"Because I can't wait any longer my love unless you want to see me lying on this cold floor, cold."

Chelimo shifted in the chair but she did not respond. Instead, she kept quiet and stared down at his strong hand holding hers on her lap. He anxiously kept his gaze on her.

"This is difficult Dane," she said looking directly into his eyes. He waited for her to continue but she did not.

"Cheli, what is difficult? Look here darling. I love you so much that nothing can get into the way of my deep feelings for you. Please speak to me," he pleaded. "By now, you should have realized that there is nothing that can stand between us. Nothing." Dane got up and walked to the coffee table. He poured a generous tot of brandy into a short glass, added some water, took a sip and came and stood in front of her.

"Honey?" he prompted. "Speak to me."

"Are you sure you want to know the truth?"

"Yes. You already know my position, that nothing can stand between us if you let me into your life."

Chelimo swallowed the lump of air that was forming around her throat. She stood up, held his hand and slowly said;

"Dane, I am circumcised."

The world seemed to stand still.

"You are what?" Dane blurted out, mouth open. He moved his hand to place the glass of brandy onto the table but missed the table. The glass collided with the hard floor, shattering into hundreds of pieces.

"I am sorry."

"What?"

Dane was in utter shock.

"I am sorry," Chelimo said looking looking down at her toes, her voice a thin whisper.

"How could you let that happen to you?"

It was an accusation yet spoken so quietly.

"Let it happen to me? Dane?"

"Yes. How?"

"How kind!"

"Aah…I mean..."

"I was too young to protest. Yes. That's how I was cut. Mutilated."

"I am sorry."

"It's alright Dane. I understand."

"What do you understand?"

"That you can't understand."

Dane shook his head and led Chelimo back to the sofa. For a while, they sat silent, fighting a war of culture. It was some minutes later that Dane managed to speak.

"Well I am sorry. I have heard about that...that horrible stuff but I must confess I have never given it much thought in this day and age. To tell you the truth,

Honey, I don't want to know about it. Look, there are things in life which some people don't want to know about. Maybe it is selfishness on my side but I am sorry."

"Now you know," Chelimo said as she walked away from him towards the door.

"Yes."

"I will leave now," she said pulling a spotless white handkerchief out of her handbag. Dane held out his hand towards her and she held it.

"Good bye my dear friend," she said. Dane did not respond. For a moment they just stood silent. Then he spoke.

"Honey, I am sorry. Truly sorry that you had to go through that barbaric ritual." He pulled her into a prolonged embrace before leading her away from the door, back to the sofa. Chelimo sobbed quietly for a while. She then looked up at Dane and said,

"Dane, from now on, you are free to find another woman, one who will make you feel like a man. That woman is not me. I will find my kind, perhaps from the hills of Kapchorwa." Chelimo begun to cry again.

Dane held her closer. He got the handkerchief from her hands and wiped her face.

"Honey don't cry. I have just been thinking. You are that woman you are sending me to go and look for. Everything you have just talked about is in the past. You can decide your future. Please don't cry."

"I know it's in the past but then, isn't the past really always with us?

"Dane, my being circumcised is not in the past. It is on me, in me, with me forever," she said quietly.

Dane drew her closer then let go of her and stood up.

"I am sorry but I will leave you now. I will make you a cup of strong Mukwano tea," said Dane.

"I knew you would leave me. I always knew it was a matter of time. You do not have to apologise," a resigned Chelimo replied. Dane turned and in one stride he stood in front of her.

"You do not understand me Cheli. You never do. So what, if you are circumcised? This practice has been going on for ages but still the girls get married, don't they? Look Cheli, I am marrying you and not that damn circumcision ritual. I have always told you that nothing will stop me from loving you. Genital cutting or none. Those men of the hills as you call them are not different from me or any other men elsewhere. Besides, you are still you. A very beautiful, loving girl with a large heart. Cheli please, say you will marry me," he pleaded. "That's the reason we are here this moment!"

She sighed and in words which he could hardly hear said. "Dane, female circumcision is different. It's not just the body. The knife takes bits of what a woman is, both on the inside and the outside. Sometimes there may be complications…" Dane, did not wait for her to complete the statement. He sought her lips and covered them with his in a deep kiss.

"The secrets of the river have caught up with me," she whispered.

"I beg your pardon?"

"Nothing."

"Why do you want to dwell on the negative? There are complications everywhere in life but we have to surmount them. Come sweetheart. Say yes, my love."

"Darling, I don't want you to regret in future and say hurtful things like 'love is blind," said Chelimo.

"Actually, love should be blind. It means that you realize each other's weaknesses but you accept one another as you are. Cheli please, don't keep on erecting roadblocks on our path to happiness. Just let go. Listen to your heart and I know your heart and mine are on the same beat! Cheli?"

"Yes, Dane I will marry you."

He dashed to his bedroom and returned with a small jewellery box.

"You almost messed up the ceremony! Here... There is always a ring." Dane giggled as he extended his hand to Chelimo. Chelimo looked at the box but did not move.

"This is what I could afford," he started apologetically. "But it is loaded with love." He opened the box, got out the ring and placed it on her finger.

Chelimo's eyes had a film of tears. They embraced for what seemed like eternity. It was Dane who broke the embrace. He walked over to the Sony player and changed the CD. Love ballads floated in the air as Chelimo melted into his chest. Her dreams were slowly coming to pass. But would Dane live to his words? To his promises?

After two months of quick preparations, Dane walked Chelimo down the aisle. They were a couple to behold - Chelimo glowing in an off-shoulder, cattle-egret white dress and Dane in a cream jacket and black trousers. There were "oohs" and "aahs" all around the church and so much goodwill for the newlyweds which made them glow even more.

Dane was a man who liked to stay within the bounds. So when it came to the moment of truth after the wedding reception was done and everybody else was gone, he had no reason to make the exception to the rules that his father's sister Millicent had given him.

The meal has three courses at the barest minimum, she had told him solemnly, though he could detect a mischievous twinkle in her eyes. Aunt Millicent was not afraid to wink rather wickedly from time to time after stressing each point and asking whether he understood. The starters – not the main course - are the most critical, Aunt Millicent had stressed. Better the starters without the main course than the main course without starters. The second course, she had said, was nothing more than a glorified or permissible rape for which the cops would impose no sanctions. The first course is what romance was made of. And the last course – if it went well – would be the most critical in ensuring that the other two would never be forgotten.

"It is the fruit and cake and whatever else that crown the night, making the dinner memorable. Miss it out and it just may be forgotten that the first two courses actually went well."

The wicked twinkle had became even more pronounced as she said that.

Aunt Millicent dwelt on the starters more than the main course "because the main course comes almost naturally and with more practice it becomes a natural. It is the starters which many men have perfected into an art but which only very few excel at. Make a mistake about the main course, but never ever compromise the starters."

Dane had listened with the earnestness of one listening to the last words of a dying dad. He listened carefully to the description of the things he was supposed to find and what to do with them. By the end of the briefing, Dane was sure he'd be able to locate the all-important shoots and what was more; he'd know just how to handle them. Dane had never exactly had a girlfriend. Raised on a strict and conservative Anglican diet, he had every faith in abstinence before marriage...and unwavering faithfulness after it. So sexually pure was he, that his close friend Joe – who did not entertain the same puritanical notions and had happily, squired one girl after another, had with a casual puff at his cigarette, declared he feared his best friend would probably insist on abstinence even after the wedding.

"God Almighty save us! And what would the poor girl do then?" another friend had exclaimed. Dane's friends had all burst into laughter.

"Some of us might have to be at standby to help," Joe had continued.

"You can if you are looking for death," another friend had said causing more laughter.

"You seem not to have noticed the transformation Dane has gone through. Even his voca. It's now; babes, honey, love, darling, eeh! Whoever thought...!"

It was until Dane promised to boycott their company that the teasing stopped.

When finally the Best Man dropped the couple off in a fine suite at the Speke Resort Munyonyo, right on the shores of Lake Victoria, it seemed the finest possible setting for the newlywed couple to get to know the joy of sex and the majesty of the wedding night. Much as Dane had been anxious for the reception to end so he could be with just his bride, the moment of truth had suddenly made him tensed up. Chelimo did not help matters either as she strutted around the room, holding this and that and speaking words that seemed sticky in her mouth.

"What are you saying?"

"That you go first in the shower," she said.

"Come on. We have to shower together."

"Eei. No. I have to sort these things first."

"Sort what? Those can wait."

"Please go," she begged. "I will bathe after you."

Dane took about five minutes in the bathroom, much of which was spent pondering on how he would kick off the proceedings between the sheets. When he finally emerged, he was fully dressed, as though he was going somewhere. His new wife murmured something about it being time to dress down, rather than up, to which they both laughed rather nervously.

"Your turn," he said, pointing to the bathroom.

"I will, shortly,"

"No. Now." It was his turn to plead.

The bride took so much time in the bathroom until Dane walked over and turned the door handle. It was secured.

"Are you okay baby?" he called out.

"Yes I am."

"You are taking too long."

"I guess I am slow because I am very tired. But I will be out shortly."

"Great."

Chelimo did not come out shortly as she had said.

Dane, fearing that something might be the matter, had to knock cautiously at the bathroom door, calling out gently. He then heard her sobbing.

"Please open for me."

"I will," she said in-between spasms of sobs.

"Now darling."

Dane spent the better part of the evening trying to coax his bride out of the bathroom. When she finally emerged, it was clear that she needed to be left alone, at least for a while.

Fortunately, Dane too was too tired and as soon as they lay on the bed, wedding fatigue took them over till the following morning.

Dane was eager to try again, but his bride was having no such thing. Although he was being the perfect gentleman, he was beginning to feel a little frustrated. On her part, Chelimo was simply afraid, not sure of what would happen. It was after supper of the second night that they both agreed they'd give it a try.

Dane understood her trauma and handled her with a gentility he never knew he possessed. He talked to her softly, caressed her wet brow and told her to relax and just let herself go with him. Much as she tried, Chelimo remained stiff with fright. She had expected Dane's love to melt away her fear. And what was more, she had thought her own strong love and desire would relax her. But in spite of his understanding and gentility, she kind of floated above her body and only felt sharp pain at the beginning as she gritted her teeth, trying to be brave about it.

You faced the knife, you can face anything else in life, the words of the old woman on circumcision night rang deep in her ear. Chelimo tried to relax and be brave but her bravery lasted only fleeting seconds, because as Dane 'descended' upon her, the image of the circumcision surgeon descending upon her with knife, ready to scoop out her switch and all that related to it, came flooding back into her memory and into her entire body. The image of the surgeon and her husband above her, were intertwined. In that confusion, panic set in. It didn't help matters when Dane made contact – the scream she withheld the day she was circumcised found this the perfect moment to go loose. Chelimo let out a piercing scream that caused both of them to recoil; one shocked and frustrated, the other frightened. Dane held her in his arms, as sobs rocked her entire body.

"It will be alright darling," he tried to console her but Chelimo was inconsolable, managing only a teary 'I am so sorry Dane,' between sobs.

Nothing happened that night and after another two days of trial and failure, both had to admit the honeymoon had been a disaster. They packed their bags and drove out of Munyonyo, to their new home in Bukoto. They were a very frustrated couple, but they held on strongly to the love strings that held them together tightly. The words, 'I am so sorry' never left Chelimo's lips all through.

It was more than a week after they left Munyonyo that they finally succeeded in consummating their marriage.

The following day they sat on their bed and talked about the sores they had both sustained in the process.

"Darling don't worry. It will get better." Dane was quick to comfort his wife.

"I really pray so," she replied, unconvinced.

Dane stood up and stood on attention. He then saluted and said, "I promise on my honour to make it better next time."

"It's not about you my dear."

"It's about me and you. This is a new journey we have embarked on and we must move on," Dane soothed. "We have only one option my love."

"I am all ears."

"To move on."

Chelimo laughed a faint laugh and buried her face into his chest. From then on, they kept trying but it never got better. Every time they tried, it proved a nightmare for Chelimo. She began to go to bed late praying and hoping that she would find Dane asleep. She loved him with all her heart but everything seemed to be spiralling out of control.

Dane had been patient for the first few months, sincerely believing that his wife was still traumatized by the knife she'd faced as a child. But he soon got impatient.

"It seems as though I married my sister," he'd declared in Joe's law chambers. "I am a very unhappy man."

On Joe's advice, they'd initially agreed on how frequent they should have sex. The lawyer that he was, Joe had insisted that the agreement be in writing - to have sex at least twice a week to avoid having to stage a fight over sex every other night, one fighting hard to get it and the other fighting equally hard to ensure it didn't happen. But it soon proved unsustainable – Chelimo complained it was painful all through, while Dane complained that he felt he was not getting the fullest benefit of his wife, beautiful though she was. When Dane returned to Joe for a periodic evaluation a month or two later, he reported that things were not yet well.

"Have you ever beaten the chick?" Joe had asked, legs up on his office table, blowing a steady stream of cigarette smoke into Dane's face, something he usually did just to irritate his best friend for the sake of it.

"I wouldn't raise a finger against the love of my life," Dane replied, shocked.

"Not even a slap?"

"No; like never."

"Then you need help," said Joe. "Learn to be a man in your own house. Your woman's stuff is your property; you paid man, you paid. You have license to do what you want with her. She shouldn't labour under the illusion that she has the option to say no. Or are you telling me she's the one wearing the trousers now?"

*****

"Our people say that a goat looks like the anthill it rubs itself against," another friend told him when he went to seek a second opinion. "If you keep Joe's company you'll begin to behave like him."

When Dane got home, he decided it was his cross to carry and he decided further that he'd not lift a finger against his wife. Somehow, he and Chelimo managed to have some kind of sex.

It was a few months after the wedding that Chelimo announced that she was pregnant. There was joy in the household that the little family was just about to be enlarged; but the joy was short-lived when it turned out that that was the end of any sexual relations between the couple. Chelimo complained of too much pain downstairs and then nausea and then something or other, each time

Dane developed any ideas. He had no choice but to slow down on the demands. After all he was enthralled about becoming a father. His happiness was immeasurable on that front. His frustration further reduced when the scan, four months down the road, proclaimed that it was a boy on the way.

Dane was excited and proud that an heir would be born into the new family at the very first time of asking.

"Although, to be frank," he added quickly. "I would have felt as equally exhilarated if it had been a girl."

"Are you being sincere?"

"Yes, I am. A child is a child," he had declared. Chelimo embraced him with loving pride. His parents too were happy when they learnt that a boy was on the way. His father spoke on and on about the importance of a boy child; pointing out that lineage and wealth of the family was preserved through male children, not females.

"The girls will give birth to children of another clan; or worse, another tribe," he explained. "And they will have basically different people altogether. If they inherit any property, our wealth will automatically go to another clan...or another tribe."

Dane tried to convince his father that a girl child was just as precious in terms of inheritance but the old man would not budge. On her part, Chelimo beamed with contentment, happy that her in-laws appreciated her. She'd heard numerous tales about the trauma of wives who couldn't get along with their in-laws, creating tension in the air and essentially turning the entire family life into a game of politics. She couldn't thank the Lord enough that she had married into a family that was so much like her parents family. She fitted in very well although she did not agree with their views, she knew there was no point in arguing with them.

"My heir!"' he would shout with joy as he caressed Chelimo's bulging stomach.

"Heir! To which throne?"asked Chelimo mockingly.

"To the Dane and Chelimo estate and throne," he teasingly told her.

It was during this time that Dane developed some discomfort while passing urine. He did not bother to tell his wife, avoiding telling her anything that might bring her anxiety. He went to see his doctor.

The doctor at Ntinda Medical Centre looked at the laboratory results and then looked at his patient, then looked at the results again.

"You have a UTI - Urinary Tract Infection, he announced, almost apologetically. "And it is looking bad – it's probably been with you for quite a while. That means I'll have to put you on a course of antibiotics for the next few days."

"No problem," replied Dane, adding that he'd be happy to pick up the drugs now as he was in a hurry to get to work.

"Not that quick," he said. "I'm afraid your spouse may also have take the same medication, because she may be having it too. So let her come and get tested."

Finally the doctor had Dane's attention.

"You mean…"

"I don't mean anything," said the doctor.

"So how does one get a UTI?"

"There are many ways," replied the old doctor. "But what is important now is for you and your partner to get medication."

Dane left the clinic angry and hurt and wasted no time in marching home. He found Chelimo in the kitchen preparing a fruit cocktail juice. He was breathing like a bull in a fight, his nostrils flaring.

"So madam holy, whose child is in your womb?" he asked in a quiet but deadly voice.

Chelimo who was five months pregnant had never seen Dane this angry. He was a stranger.

"What do you mean?" she turned around, more in surprise than in anger. He got out the medical form, showed it to her and demanded to know who she had been sleeping with.

Chelimo burst into tears and swore to high heaven she had never been touched by any other man save her husband.

"The Lord is my witness. But how can you even have such a thought when you know what I have been going through with you?" she sobbed. Dane looked into his wife's eyes and the innocence therein smote his heart. He regretted his rash reaction. After an hour of talking, they agreed to go back to Dr. Medard.

At the doctor's Chelimo admitted she had had a UTI before – from time to time, as matter of fact –ever since she was about 18 and yes, she also had extremely painful menstrual periods that had become particularly aggravated since she was 18.

Looking knowingly at her maiden name, Dr. Medard, rather apologetically, asked her if she had been circumcised. The couple both looked down. The answer was obvious. The doctor nodded several times, indicating that several things were now becoming clear.

"This is a common condition among circumcised women," he said. "You are not the only one."

"Why, doctor? I believe most circumcised women do not have multiple sexual partners. How come then?"

"The UTI usually occurs because of the narrowing of the urinary outlet which prevents the complete emptying of urine from the bladder. And many women like that suffer very painful menstruation periods because there's a build-up of urine and blood in the uterus, leading to inflammation of the bladder and internal sexual organs." The UTI can also be picked from a toilet seat.

It was the young couple's turn to nod and nod, as they began to put two and two together.

"And I must add that the other common condition that stays with most of them throughout their lives is extreme pain during sexual intercourse, bringing couples both physical discomfort and psychological trauma."

Dane turned and looked at Chelimo.

"Doctor, what my wife suffers cannot be described a mere discomfort. Hers is something else!"

"I understand," the doctor said twisting his head into an attentive posture.

"The pain inflicted by FGM does not stop with the initial procedure as the girls are always told. It always continues as ongoing torture throughout a woman's life," said the doctor thoughtfully, eyes on the ceiling as though the answers were written up there.

"Then doctor, why has it continued unabated?" Dane asked.

"Many women volunteer because they seek social acceptance and community validation; for without that, their lives can take a difficult turn. But truth is that the procedure causes almost irreparable trauma. So while the women may enjoy the validation and acceptance from the society around them, they have to live with personal discomfort, and to fight a battle that they will never win. You see, sex is both a physical and a psychological exercise and both domains must be comfortable in order for the woman, and even the man, to enjoy it. But circumcision intrudes on both domains and successfully kills any chance of enjoyment in most women. This leads to long-term effects that the women can never fully cope with or overcome."

"The question as my husband has already asked is why it has continued to thrive despite all these challenges?"

"Nobody has the answer. There is still more. Women may experience chronic pain, chronic pelvic infections, development of cysts, abscesses and genital ulcers, excessive scar tissue formation, infection of the reproductive system, decreased sexual enjoyment and psychological consequences, such as post-traumatic stress disorder. Even more surprising is that the male partner can also experience pain and related complications."

Dane and Chelimo looked at each other.

"The combined physical and psychological stress causes women to be tense and contract the muscles around the vagina. Any penetration will therefore be painful and even the mere thought of it will cause pain to the woman even long before she is touched," he concluded.

"Is that what happens to every circumcised woman?" Dane asked.

"Yes. A few cases maybe different but the majority go through that."

"I am sorry doctor, but why then do women let it happen to their daughters?" Dane asked again.

"Culture can be the worst form of imprisonment. That's why it is important for our communities to discard negative and harmful cultural practices and retain the positive aspects only." The doctor's steady stare indicated he was done with them.

Both Dane and Chelimo looked at each other and then looked away, unwilling to meet the doctor's eye again.

As they drove back home, they were both quiet. Dane moved his left hand from the steering wheel and found his wife's hand. She squeezed it and let his arm lie on her lap.

"Honey, am so sorry," she said to him.

"It's not your fault. Just know that I will always love you. There is more to marriage than frequent sex. I love you Cheli."

Chelimo's throat constricted. A film of tears covered her eyes. Dane's understanding had touched her to the core. She hoped he would always understand since circumcision was a life-time challenge.

"Darling, I will forever be grateful that I got such a lovely husband."

"Honey don't be grateful. You are the best wife any man could dream of."

Dane engaged low gear and indicated a left turn, stalling just briefly to let oncoming traffic pass, before easing the car through the gate and onto the driveway. They were back home.

Chapter Eight

Everything seemed just fine when she was admitted into the maternity suite at Mulago Hospital on a Thursday night. She checked into a private room with all the facilities that she could wish for. She lowered herself – with Dane's help – onto what proved to be a strong bed with a mattress soft but firm. Chelimo was in extreme pain and thought she was due any moment, although nothing happened for the next two days. False labour, is what the midwives called it. They dismissed her without further thought, advising her to return home and wait for the actual labour.

The young couple decided it would be better to wait from the hospital, as there was no telling which emergency could arise and cause problems. The cost of extra payment for the room would be nothing big compared to the price they'd pay if anything, God forbid, went wrong.

It was on Saturday when she felt the labour pains return but by Sunday she had not delivered yet and she felt like she could not bear it anymore. She asked Dane to call the midwife on duty.

The midwife who was having lunch told Dane – rather nonchalantly – that Chelimo was not yet ready. And she was so rude; Dane felt a chill down his spine and he did not want to belabour himself with undue protestations. As the contractions rocked her body, Chelimo twisted and cried, but the midwife was nowhere to be seen. Being her first time in the labour suite, Chelimo was not sure what was going on and felt she had no choice but to trust the midwife, even though a nagging doubt lingered at the back of her mind.

Half an hour later her doubts were validated when she felt the baby coming down. Dane ran to fetch the midwife who came reluctantly, a full 10 minutes later, quarrelling about patients who thought they knew more than the medics. But she too had to admit she had made a horrible misjudgement when she saw the baby's head peeping. Chelimo was rushed to the labour suite but even though the baby seemed eager to get out, the process proved difficult.

It was after the nurses made a big cut on her to widen the tight passage that the baby finally came out almost breathless. The boy cried just once and kept quiet – even though the assisting midwife made effort to slap him on the small pink buttocks. A few minutes later she noticed that he was not breathing. No matter how hard they tried to resuscitate him, he neither cried nor breathed. After an hour of struggle, the second midwife shrugged her shoulders and declared the inevitable. The baby was dead. The nurse wrapped the still baby in the beautiful linens that Dane had brought home one evening. Dane and Chelimo were numb throughout the entire process.

When the gynaecologist finally showed up, he listened carefully to both the nurse and Dane before he ruled that Chelimo's tightness had worn the baby out as he tried to push his way through. He said that there had been a few other cases like that but that they were not many.

"Otherwise two days of labour is normal," said the doctor, gently. "That is why the nurses had not called me yet. Some people even go into the third day and they still produce normally."

"He didn't fight for his life," declared the midwife. "That's the problem with boys. Had it been a girl she would have survived. The girls always fight and never give up."

Chelimo and Dane did not respond, neither did the doctor.

At the funeral in Kabale, the two went through the motions like zombies on assignment. Even when they returned to Kampala, life appeared in no hurry to return to normal.

Dane was so disconcerted after the death of the boy that when his mother confided in him that Chelimo was an unlucky girl he had no energy to defend his wife or even to object even though he knew that all this was rubbish.

"It's such a misfortune to lose a first born baby. And a boy. There's always a next time nevertheless," his mother reassured him.

The next time took quite a while to come. After the initial trauma of losing a first child had worn off, Dane was enthusiastic between the sheets. Chelimo however showed no such interest. She was withdrawn, said little and complained of pain all the times they made love. It didn't help matters one bit when Chelimo's mother – who'd been in and out of hospital for a while, died.

Talking to her a few days earlier, Chelimo had had no reason to suspect anything was amiss. Her mother had sounded fairly strong and back on her feet. Then they called that her situation had worsened again. Chelimo sent a driver to bring her to Kampala and when they carried out the tests, it was cervical cancer already in its advanced stages. Chelimo's mother then revealed that sometimes she would have pus coming from her private parts but she just kept it to herself because she was ashamed of talking about it. She said she thought it was a sickness of being sexually loose and since she wasn't, she hadn't known how to explain it. A few weeks in hospital could not do anything. She died a painful death.

Chelimo, who had always seen her mother as an eternal and immovable bastion of strength and courage was completely shattered. She was totally numb as they went through the funeral motions and barely stayed sane. Luckily for her, Dane was supportive and by her side through it all. Chelimo was also greatly helped by Mrs. Orono, head of the Mothers Union at St. Luke Church, Ntinda, who stood stoutly by her through the pain.

The mood in the household improved when Chelimo announced that she was pregnant again.

*****

She endured two days of painful labour, an experience that once again reminded her of the painful circumcision knife years back and of the loss of her first baby. Chelimo felt as though the knife had been reapplied, but this time for a prolonged period. She wept until she could weep no more.

Eventually, the doctor declared he would perform a caesarean operation on her, now that labour had proved problematic again.

"We do not want to take another chance. I had hoped that after the first child, you would now produce normally but that might not be the case."

"That's okay Doctor. I am ready for the operation," Chelimo whispered.

"Do you want to come into theatre with her?"

"Yes Doctor," Dane said stepping forward.

"I don't think so Dane. Please stay outside but do not go far." Chelimo said. She did not want Dane to see the operation. "It might be a traumatizing experience for you."

Dane paced back and forth in front of the theatre as he waited for the operation to get done with. He called a few friends and asked them to pray for his dear wife and their baby. Although it did not take long, for Dane it took eternity. When the Midwife finally emerged out of theatre with the good news, Dane was covered in perspiration.

"What shall we call this child, my love?" he asked his wife as he sat by her side.

Chelimo didn't think twice about the name. She called her Daisy Chemtai, after her best friend whose life had been cut short by the knife, one of the untold secrets of the river.

*****

The bad news didn't properly hit Chelimo until a few days later when she woke up to find herself covered in urine. Initially she dismissed it as a one-off and went back to rest after a good clean up but when she was awakened by the now familiar feel of wetness, Chelimo was shocked. The shock increased when she found that she could no longer control her urine - it leaked continually; forcing Chelimo to visit the nearest supermarket for adult pampers. Not many supermarkets stocked adult pampers and many an attendant frowned and wondered why an adult would require a pamper. Embarrassed, she moved from one supermarket to another until she finally found what she was looking for.

A few days later, Chelimo mastered the courage to talk about her dilemma to Dane. The following day they went shopping - this time for a doctor. They decided Dr. Medard would do.

The doctor didn't need a whole day to establish what had happened. He listened carefully to her story of the last few days and then nodded his head in understanding.

"What is the problem doctor?"

"I am sorry but the difficult labour has done more harm to you than we had thought. It has left you with what we call vesicovaginal fistula. Your system is damaged."

"What does all that mean doctor?"

"What that means is that your system is free flowing. Uncontrollable. Haven't you heard of anything called vaginal fistula?

"Hmm...Yes...but not quite sure what it is."

"Fistula is a hole."

"Hmm."

"Vesicovaginal fistula is an obstetrical condition. When the wall of the bladder is raptured, it eats into the vagina; thereby causing urine to flow through the vagina instead of the urethra which is otherwise the normal route.

"In that condition a person cannot control her urine, so it just leaks all the time. This is often after complicated childbirth especially when adequate medical care is not available. In simple terms, it has been described to be caused by prolonged labour, where the sustained pressure of the baby's head on the mother's pelvic bone damages soft tissues around childbirth canal, creating a hole between the vagina and the bladder. The pressure deprives blood flow to the tissue and eventually, the tissue dies and comes away, leaving a fistula, which leads to constant leaking of urine through the vagina."

"Is that what I am suffering from doctor?"

"Yes. That is what you suffered from and that is the impact you are suffering now. If the gynaecologist had carried out an elective caesarean section, it would never have happened. And it is worse for circumcised women, because they have scant elasticity, which heightens the possibility for fistulas. So you see, you had no chance.

"We shall carry out one more test," the doctor said.

"Which one? And what for?"

"I'd like to rule out cervical cancer, even while we are still coming to terms with fistula."

Chelimo bowed her head, shocked to the marrow as she remembered her mother. After a while the doctor began to explain himself.

"The link between circumcision, obstructed labour and lacerations to the cervix is now established and this chain is known to greatly increase the risk of cervical cancer," he began slowly. "Once identified early, cervical cancer can be treated." Chelimo looked up.

"The problem with our poor countries is that most women - especially those in the rural areas - is that they come to hospital when it is almost too late. And sometimes of course they may not easily access the necessary medical care. And it has also been established that circumcised women are at a higher risk of cervical cancer. But I suspect you are safe Chelimo. The test is for 'just in case', just to rule it out."

It was at this point that Chelimo held her head in her palms and begun to weep. She was not weeping for herself but for her best friend Chemtai, long dead; her mother, more recently gone and she wept at the helplessness she felt at the realization that *rotwet* had taken from her the people that she loved most. *Rotwet* had also taken her own happiness. The *rotwet*, whose only preoccupation and passion was to take and take without ever giving anything worthwhile in return except pain, was not yet done with her. Chelimo did not want to think about what else the *rotwet* was about to take from her.

Dane pulled her towards him and held her in his arms. The doctor left them for a while until Chelimo's sobs died out.

"You will be safe Chelimo," he began.

"But how can my people be so callous doctor? Is is there a reason women are being punished thus? Maybe something in history that we do not know about?"

"I doubt," the doctor said. "Female circumcision is considered by its practitioners to be an essential part of raising a girl properly. They think that it ensures pre-marital virginity and inhibits extra-marital sex, because it reduces a woman's libido. But the truth is that it's too harsh not only to the woman but even to those around her. We shall take samples now. You need to go back and rest."

Dane nodded gravely as the doctor spoke. The pieces of the strange puzzle were starting to come together; the twists in this rather unusual paradox were beginning to unwind, little by little. He said nothing on the way home; simply preferring to hold his poor wife's hand. Chelimo was too distraught to offer any opinions and continued to feel at fault for making Dane miserable and unable to enjoy a marriage he had clearly looked forward to. *Rotwet*'s harvest was costly and heavy.

A few days later, the doctor was pleased to call Chelimo with good news for a change, as he confirmed that the tests had not shown any signs of cancerous cells. He also gave her a reference to experts he thought could handle the fistula. Two pieces of good news. For the first time in a long time, Chelimo smiled.

*****

The shock of the onset of fistula hit the household terribly hard and adjustments had to be made. The most painful was that Dane insisted on separate bedrooms and even though he tried his best to cover up, it was obvious he had begun shunning her. Living in shame and isolation in her husband's home was humiliation *par excellence* for Chelimo and she wept every day.

The doctors advised that although the fistula condition was treatable, she would have to wait a few weeks to enable healing of her initial scars from the caesarean operation to heal before subjecting her to another operation.

Over the next few months Chelimo underwent three surgeries to repair the damage, but none were successful. Heartbroken, she returned home to her child…and to her husband, who did not seem to take much interest in her. Her spirit and hope were subdued and she decided to accept her fate. She resigned herself to the use of adult diapers and smiled wryly whenever she went shopping – buying pampers for the baby and then for its mother. She smiled even wider when she dressed her daughter first and then herself. She moved less and less, interacted on the social scene even less and kept more to herself.

Daisy however was a bundle of joy and energy, always lighting up Dane and Chelimo's world. She brought a new joy into the family that was otherwise completely devoid of any pretence to happiness. The new parents found it easier to get along with each other with Daisy as the uniting factor. But every time they focused on each other there was no end of trouble. Both became more and more withdrawn, each walking and wandering about in their own world, only intersecting around Daisy.

It was during that period that Dane met Sarah; a workmate at the Uganda Revenue Authority who said 'yes' even before he had asked for any favours.

Dane had long resisted the temptation to go "extra-curricular" as one of his teachers used to refer to it, his Christian upbringing keeping him in check. He felt he had not taken vows for nothing and for a long while felt that this was the latter aspect of "for better for worse." He felt under duty to stick to his wife and support her all through.

But the attentions of Sarah, a cute, light-skinned girl with a smile that curved her lips into a small opening rose flower, slowly caused him to lower his guard. Even though Dane hated to admit it, Sarah was delightful company. When she – for the hundredth time - suggested coffee at her apartment one evening, Dane obliged. It took only two and a half coffees. To be precise, the third was abandoned midway as they made a mad dash for her bedroom. That was the beginning of his late returns home and even much less interest in every aspect of his home, with the exception of his daughter.

*****

Chelimo's instinct told her something was afoot and she was not sure which torture was better –the painful sex encounter, or his complete disinterest in the marriage, punctuated by his late nights out. Dane had turned into Mr. Walk-about who wandered home only when it was inevitable. She hated to admit that the marriage was over and done with. But she decided not to give it up. She truly loved Dane and believed that deep in his heart, he too still loved her.

*****

It was two years later that Dr. Medard alerted Chelimo about the Centre for Reproductive Health and Fistula Repair in Mbale; a private facility run by a quartet of youthful doctors who were famed for brilliance and their knack for adventurous surgery. Overwhelmed by the burden of her condition, she decided to seek help. The doctors were of the view that her case was so complicated that it would need a skilful and experienced fistula specialist to operate on her. They said that circumcision often tended to make treatment of an obstetric fistula more complicated, because the scar tissue resulting from cutting usually made fistula repair surgery more difficult.

"You might get well if you are lucky but it can't even be described as a fifty/fifty trial. It's almost a ninety to ten; as the Englishmen would put it, it's pound to penny, nothing more, I'd say," said Dr. Musani, the team leader.

"What do you mean doctor?"

"Your chance to get well is just about ten percent."

"What are my chances if I don't do it? Can the condition heal on it's own?"

"Your chance at not doing it is that you will not suffer with surgery wounds. And no, this kind of fistula can't heal on its own."

"I will take the ten percent risk. I will do it doctor."

Chelimo made an appointment with Dr. Musani. "This is my last chance," she told herself. She cried like a child throughout the first day at the hospital; partly because of the suffering and shame that she had been living with for so long and also from her embarrassment during the examination of her fistula. She felt the entire procedure was too intimate for her liking, but she was spurred on by the promise and possibility of a life free from the stigma and pain of fistula.

*****

When she recovered from the drugs and the doctors

told her that the operation was successful, the doctors were surprised when she begun to cry again instead of celebrate.

"Why?"

She did not respond. She wondered how she would communicate the news to Dane. In the end she decided she would tell him anyway.

When she finally announced the good news to him - after three months - he seemed genuinely delighted, though he appeared to be in no hurry to make a fuss about it. On her part though, Chelimo saw this as the perfect chance to restore her marriage…and hopefully have her husband return to their bedroom. Although she had not missed anything by way of sex – she still didn't think much about it – she had missed him. Chelimo decided that she'd allow him to have all the sex he wanted, no matter how dull, painful and routine the entire process was, if at all that would keep the marriage alive.

After a deep conversation with Mrs Orono after the weekly Mothers Union fellowship at St. Luke Church - the elderly lady had become a second mother to Chelimo since her own mother passed on - Chelimo felt positive. "What will make all the difference will start within you," Mrs. Orono had told her over and over.

As Dane's birthday was close by, Chelimo thought it the perfect occasion to resurrect what was in essence a marriage that had died years back. They usually went for dinner on their birthdays but for this one, Chelimo had proposed they have a quiet one at home. Dane loved home-made food - millet bread, sweet potatoes, or steamed bananas with mixed vegetables, peas, beans, eggplant and the like. He was not a rice person or what he called 'those wormy little things' - which Chelimo insisted was an uncharitable description of Spaghetti. His favourites were millet, vegetables mixed with groundnut and sim-sim paste. If he was to eat meat, it had to be smoked first before being boiled in a pot. Same for chicken and fish. Nothing fresh. He was not much of an eater. Not that he didn't have the appetite but he was watching his weight and minding the health implications of certain types not to mention amounts of food. He was happy that his wife was the same.

He agreed to the proposal and so they had dinner at home. Chelimo had cooked all the dishes herself. She had sent for smoked fish from her village, knowing that it was done better back home. She had taken her usual evening shower and wrapped herself in a colourful kanga cloth. She picked a black camisole with spaghetti straps with a low neck. Usually while at home relaxing, she never wore a bra. Childbirth had mercifully not left her with overly large breasts and the camisole accentuated her beautiful bosom. She had cut off her hair when her son died and always wore it short. Dane had complimented her so generously that Chelimo decided even though she had gone short hair in mourning, it would remain her thing. She sprayed herself with a whiff of "Kenzo," the perfume he always bought for her.

When he came in around nine o'clock, he looked

a bit tired and there was something else in his eyes which she could not read. She was sitting on the corner sofa listening to their favourite jazz music and had switched off all the lights save for the big lamp stand, whose bulb gave just enough mood light.

"Hi honey. Welcome back home and happy birthday," Chelimo said as she hugged him. She let her lips seek out his and she held on longer than she ever remembered, her tongue touching and teasing his. She was surprised to smell a whiff of alcohol on him. He rarely touched alcohol when they had special appointments. Well, it's his birthday, thought Chelimo. It's okay after all, for a man to indulge himself on his birthday. She smiled as she led him to his favourite chair and gave him a glass of his mixed fruit juice which he gulped down.

"Let me go shower," he said as he threw off his coat and started unknotting the tie.

Once he left, he took rather long to return from the shower. Chelimo went to check on him only to find the bathroom empty. She went to the bedroom and found him sprawled on the bed, a towel tied loosely around his waist. He was already in a deep slumber.

She shook him gently.

"Uh?" he grunted.

"Darling, it's time for dinner," she whispered.

He grunted and reluctantly got up. He opened the wardrobe, got out a polo T-shirt and pair of jeans and dressed up.

He joined Chelimo on the table and she served

him his favourite fish parts.

Chelimo was at her most cheerful. Chatting away, cracking jokes which he politely laughed at. She could tell however, that his heart had drifted away. She pretended and went on as if she hadn't noticed anything was amiss.

"Time for bed darling," Chelimo winked suggestively at Dane. "And the silver lining to the birthday cake," she cooed as she seductively rubbed herself against him. She was not sure but thought she heard him grunt some kind of trepidation. She held his hands and led him to their comfortable bed. Today, she was ready to take the lead.

She smiled to herself as she started taking off his T-shirt , determined to make it work. After all, she was still deeply in love with him. Yes she had resolved to be brave in the face of pain so as to make Dane happy.

When everything was warm and cosy, she lowered the bed side lamp and reached for him, but Dane who was determined not to touch Chelimo anymore hoisted himself from the bed, turned the lamp to the brightest and stared down at her nakedness.

"Chelimo, it's not your fault. And I don't hold it against you but…" he hesitated. She noticed that since they first met at the Bachelors Party, it was the first time he was calling her by her full name - Chelimo.

"Yes Dane," she responded in a small voice, hesitant and insecure.

"Look Chelimo, we can't go on like this. I can't

take it anymore. I'm not sure whether you can either. Let's face the reality now. It is over."

"Say that again?" Her ears tingled.

"This is a marriage that never should have been," he said, his voice stable and strong, his eyes avoiding Chelimo's. She swallowed although there was nothing in her mouth. She struggled with nothingness as it pressed against the walls of her throat, momentarily disabling her speech. Dane continued.

"You remember what you told me when I proposed to marry you?"

"Yes...I do...remember..." she stuttered.

"You were right."

"That's not what you said then."

"I know. A man can always get wiser. That's not a crime. Besides, we both know the truth. I am not inventing what I am saying."

"Surely Dane, there is more to marriage than sex. Look, we love each other. We have a lovely daughter and I am sure we will get more children. I don't want to call it quits because I know I love you. You know I love you despite the challenges we have gone through. And look here, Dane, we don't want our daughter to grow up without the guidance of her father. More so, when her father is alive and like I have said, we will have more children. I am ready for anything that will keep our marriage together. Please Dane, we have always supported each other through all these challenges. You can't think of divorce now," she pleaded. "We can live together as a happy couple again if we both give it a try."

"Try, my foot! Chelimo, I am not living. I am merely existing! And you too have been a very sad woman. I'm sure you will find happiness elsewhere once we go separate ways."

She laughed, her lips half twisted, half open, quivering as if they desperately needed an invisible hand to hold them together and close them. The fact that he was dead serious was beginning to sink in. And, he had called her Chelimo a second time.

"Look Dane, do you also remember that you promised on your honour that my circumcision would have no impact on our relationship? On your love to be more specific?" Dane was silent.

"Do you remember? You saluted on your promise. Remember?" He did not respond. Instead he laughed unnecessarily loud, startling even himself, for he looked around the room, eyes darting here and there, as if to confirm that he was alone with Chelimo and that no one had heard him laugh. His mouth hang open long after he stopped laughing as if he was about to swallow a big chunk of food.

"My friend, the problem you have is not one to be brushed aside," he jabbed at her as he got up and started dressing.

She stared at him.

"My dear girl, we both know that I have tried my best over the years and I simply can't go on.

"We have both tried Dane."

"And?" he said raising his arms in the air. "To be honest, and I do not mean to be mean; your switch is off, Chelimo; there's no trace of electricity flowing within. The lights are all out. Let's not pretend it's not dark in here."

Chelimo lowered her head, as tears streamed down her face. She said nothing.

"Those women should have told you the day they took you through the secrets of the river; that when you take the switch off, the current goes with it," he said as he opened the door.

"Let's be fair to each other. You also know that I tried, my dear Chelimo."

"Wait Dane, we can solve this. I know we can. Where are you going?"

"I've tried. And age is already catching up with us. With me. I have only one life to live; and I won't live it like this. But always remember, I tried."

Chelimo sat glued onto the bed as Dane strode purposefully to the door, opened it, walked through calmly and then banged it shut, sending an echo ringing through the house. When the echo subsided Chelimo, in a daze, listened to his footsteps grow faint and fainter. Presently she heard the living room door open and it was quickly followed by another loud bang as he shut it. She could no longer hear his footsteps. She sat still waiting. Hoping. Praying. Then she heard it. The unmistakable sound of his car starting, gasping and then easing into a dull whiiiiizzz, as Dane made his way out of his home.

Out of their lives.

There was a heavy silence as reality sank in.

Chelimo was about to crumble when the soft voice of her daughter brought her back to her senses. She had not heard her bedroom door re-open after Dane's exit.

"Mummy?" It was Daisy approaching her, rubbing her sleepy eyes.

"Yes my baby?" Chelimo responded as she swept her into her arms. She was her world.

"Where is Daddy?"

"Daddy isn't here yet. He has gone to pick ice-cream for you," Chelimo said without thinking.

"I love Daddy," she said as she jumped into their bed.

Chelimo blinked away the fresh flow of tears that threatened to pour out again.

She would probably take her to visit Quality Supermarket which was her daughter's favourite local supermarket. She would then let her chose her own ice cream. As long as she wanted it.

Suddenly a fresh anger consumed Chelimo and she wondered why Dane had done that to her and their beautiful Daisy.

"Are you for real Dane?" Chelimo found herself asking.

"Yeees Mummy?" It was Daisy asking.

"Sssh. Sleep baby. I will wake you up when dad comes."

"Good night Mummy."

She slid into bed next to her daughter and reached for the switch on the wall. She wanted darkness. She did not want to see anything.

Chelimo's lips twisted into a smile as the light went off. Clearly, their marriage switch too had gone off. She found her daughter's hand and held it until the break of dawn. A new life, a new routine had set in.

In the morning, Chelimo put her pillows out in the sun to dry. She was surprised at how deep a human being's reservoir for tears was.

*****

Interestingly through common friends, Chelimo got all the news of what was happening between Dane and Sarah. Dane had straight away moved into Sarah's house. It did not take him long to start complaining that Chelimo had been a better wife than Sarah by far. Whereas she had cherished and respected him as a husband, Sarah went about her business like she was doing him a favour by being his wife.

"Why then doesn't he come back? Our door is open." Chelimo had told the bearer of the news.

"Because he now has no complaints in the bedroom. He says that Sarah is everything he had never seen in a woman, never mind she is only the second woman he has known."

Dane had also not hidden his view that Sarah's enthusiasm in the dead of night was amazing - she moaned to his every touch and purred like a contented cat. The nights were too short! Finally, Dane let out, Aunt Millicent's advice had began to make sense and that he was surprised it had taken him this long to figure out why his life was not a happy one. He still thought a lot about his wife, he admitted but said he had discovered how much he had missed out in marrying her. Dane was also consumed with the paradox that while Sarah made him feel like a man, it was Chelimo who made him feel like a husband.

"That's enough. Please stop there," Chelimo had told the bearer of the dead news.

"But he misses you. He misses Daisy terribly although he is determined to begin a new life. Besides he says he cannot bear to return considering the way he left."

"I said stop. Please. That's enough."

Chelimo sobbed worse than she did the night he left her. She knew then that she had to uproot and throw over the fence all the hopes that she had nursed. Dane was never going to return into her life.

*****

For Chelimo the separation was as painful as *rotwet*, if not more so (she couldn't make up her mind which was to be preferred). Chelimo was into the life she had never anticipated - bringing up her child without a father. Both mother and child could often be found crying – the child because so many things had changed in her life and she terribly missed her father; and Chelimo, because she didn't know what to do. Those were the moments she wished her mother was still alive.

She sought opinions from different people and discovered that there were as many opinions as there were people she consulted. Each one gave an opinion depending on what experiences they had gone through. It was all up to Chelimo to fathom which solution would fit her circumstances better.

"I have failed to come to terms with the situation," she told her close friends. "It is painful when I know he is there somewhere, breeding with some other woman, while I, who gave him everything I could is left with nothing in my arms."

And she had Daisy to look after. No matter how much she tried to comfort her, Daisy was inconsolable. Chelimo decided Daisy would not go to boarding school. She would let her stay home until she decided on her own to move out maybe after University.

Her friends advised her to get another man but she shunned them off. That thought never crossed her mind, not even once. It's a fool whose sheep escapes a secoond time, she told herself.

Chelimo transferred every bit of love she had invested in Dane, to her daughter. She built her life around Daisy. More importantly, she determined that she would from then on do whatever was within her means to stop any other Sabiny girl from undergoing the same pain she had suffered. And that she would succeed in life, marriage or no marriage. An anthill that is destined to become a giant anthill will definitely become one, no matter how many times it is destroyed by elephants, she constantly reminded herself.

*****

The years crept by. Chelimo decided to join politics.

"Since when did you become a politician?" her friends asked her.

"I genuinely want to serve my people to the best of my ability," she told them.

"But in which constituency are you going to stand?"

"I have two options. I can either stand in my maiden constituency where I am born or in the constituency where I am married. Remember I and Dane are not officially divorced. So I am still his wife legally."

She was surprised at how Dane's name had become like any other name. It no longer had the ability to cause her any pain. She was pleased with herself for the way she had managed to cope.

"But I will not stand in Dane's constituency. I will stand where I was born. After all, I did not live long in Dane's home. The people there will say I'm not living with their son so I can't represent them in Parliament. I will therefore go to Kapchorwa. After all my people in Kapchorwa need me more than the people in Kabale. Those women need me."

In Kapchorwa she was humbled by the

overwhelming support. Everybody welcomed her with open arms.

"Our educated girl is back to serve us. We shall give her our vote," most people told her opponents.

The old people were ecstatic.

"Our girl went through the secrets of the river. She has the mark of the leopard. She is a true girl of the tribe and will uphold our cultural values. We shall therefore vote for her," they clapped.

*****

She went through a smooth election and scored a landslide victory. When the President announced a new cabinet, Chelimo was thrilled that she was invited to be on board as the Minister for Environment, a position she embraced and graced with diligence and distinction. She was even more thrilled when, two years later, following a cabinet reshuffle, she was given the Culture portfolio. It was a fresh challenge and a welcome distraction seeing that it came soon after she had quietly divorced Dane.

Chelimo threw her soul and all into her work and soon Dane became a faint memory. Later she heard that he and his new wife Sarah had moved to Gulu in Northern Uganda where Dane, on promotion, was now head of the currency centre. She didn't care. But she was happy that occasionally Dane would call Daisy and Daisy would be so enthralled. And eventually, he started sending money for her school fees. Not that Chelimo could not afford to provide for her daughter but it made Daisy happy to know that her father cared about her. Whatever made her baby happy made Chelimo happy.

*****

Chelimo was brought back to the present by the raindrops pelting on the body of the vehicle they were travelling in.

"Have those hooligans harmed my daughter?" she asked the driver.

"We are almost there madam," the driver responded. Under normal circumstances the Minister would have told him that's why he always failed exams but these were not normal circumstances whichever way you looked at it. So she simply ignored what she thought was a stupid answer.

"Oh Daisy, I am sending you this message: you can't see me but I am with you. Wherever you are sweetheart, just know that mummy is by your side. Daisy can you hear me?"

"Madam, God is with your daughter. He will save her. Just let His will be done," the driver said again.

Chelimo could tell that the man was just talking to comfort her. When you believe, you do not say let God's will be done. You state what you believe. What you want God to do, she thought.

Chapter Nine

Daisy was in another world. The old woman who had taken charge of her was now talking to her.

"Child, take off your clothes..."

Daisy did not. Instead she held her uniform close to her body.

"Look, we have clothes for you for the ceremony. Come child, we don't have much time on our hands." Daisy only stared at her like one hypnotized. She did not move.

The old woman held Daisy's dress and pulled it off. "You don't want your uniform soiled," she continued. Daisy was surprised by the energy that hid in the old woman's pale hands. She looked at the nerves stretching across the back of the hands and the unkempt nails. She shifted her eyes to her small thighs that now lay bare under the woman's hands.

The woman quickly moved her hand to Daisy's panty and begun to tug at it. Daisy protested and her hands automatically moved to keep the panty in place. The old woman gently pried away Daisy's hands and brought the panty down. Daisy shivered with apprehension. The old woman then brought a wrapper and tied it around Daisy's body. She then led her outside for a bath. With the first slap of the very cold water on to her body, Daisy swallowed her breath and jumped several feet into the air, her mind back home at the warm water in her bathroom.

"What's your problem?" the old woman asked.

"Cold water."

The old woman laughed and explained. "Child, cleansing water is never warmed. This water is straight from the river and these herbs are from the womb of the earth."

She held the herbs with both hands and started scrubbing Daisy as if she had not bathed for a year. Daisy shivered like a leaf in the wind, teeth chattering in a mad dance. After the ritual was over, the old woman led her back inside the hut and gave her a blanket, showing her where she was to spend what was left of the night. Daisy had now stopped resisting. She followed the instructions.

"Here, take this hot cup of sweet herbs. You must be hungry," the old woman said extending the steaming mug to Daisy. She stared at the old woman as she received the mug. The old woman sighed and shook her head.

"We will get up at the croak of the cock - that hour when the earth is quiet and you can hear it breathe. Then we shall go to the river. Sleep well child," ended the old woman.

Daisy did not respond. She wondered how the old woman could possibly bring herself to wish her a good night. Did she think Daisy was a stone of sorts? A wild tree? A river flowing with the natural terrain? She placed the mug with its untouched contents down and turned and faced the wall and prayed that her mother would find her before the cock croaked.

The old woman lay down on the mat in the corner and the other three who had hitherto been silent watchers, all this while, followed suit.

A deep quiet descended on the hut. The only noise Daisy could hear was the soft snoring of the old women.

Daisy remained wide awake huddled in the blanket that the old woman had offered her. In her entire life, she had known only one sleepless night - when their neighbour died back in Kampala. She'd been so overwhelmed by the fear of death that she failed to sleep. She'd tiptoed to her mother's bed and slept shortly after. Tonight she was all alone, stuck with three old women who she was scared of. Outside rain gushed down from the heavens with an anger that could be felt in the whizzing wind and the breaking tree branches.

*****

"This rain is so heavy," Chelimo was telling the driver.

"Madam, I don't remember it raining this heavily in Kapchorwa in the last ten or so years.. Actually I do not remember such rain at all. I remember my father telling us about the worst rains in this part. That was about forty years ago. It washed away some of the highest hills and the destruction was terrible."

"Do you come from Kapchorwa?"

"Yes I do."

"What a coincidence."

"It's not. They wanted somebody who understands the terrain."

Just then, Chelimo's cell phone rang. It was the IGP.

"Madam Minister, we are making good progress but the rain is so heavy, we have to slow down. Unfortunate I daresay, because we suspect these people who kidnapped the girl must be determined to circumcise her and..."

"Please don't say it. Please," Chelimo said in a vehement but fright-filled voice.

"Madam, we have to face reality if we are to save the girl from the knife. Like I was saying, we think they plan to carry out the ritual early in the morning. Not only is it the day you were circumcised but also they cannot afford to keep the girl for so long because I am sure they know we are on their track."

"But if that is what you suspect, how can you say we are making good progress? What I see is that we are instead running short of time!"

"I know. It's this rain. Why the heavens had to open up tonight of all nights is something that has beaten my understanding. The meteorological department had promised us a fairly dry day and night!"

There was a moment of silence then the Minister heard the IGP ask.

"What's the matter?" the IGP barked in the phone.

"What's the matter?" the Minister re-echoed but there was no response.

"I asked, what's the matter driver?"

"Sir, the road is blocked!"

"Roadblock?"

"No. There has been a massive landslide!"

"Oh no!" the minister heard the IGP exclaim.

"Sir, you are stepping off the vehicle without protection. You must put on a rain-coat Sir."

"Oh no!" the IGP repeated over and over.

Chelimo had listened to everything. The IGP had continued speaking to his driver without switching off the phone. Chelimo's car drew closer and stopped behind the IGP's which had already parked. She quickly jumped out ignoring her driver's protests.

When she realised exactly how deep her predicament was, she burst into tears, wailing like one demented, startling everybody.

"Too late, too late! Oh God, please protect my child!"

"Madam, please calm down. Yes, I know this is terrible. For sure, if these gods had not decided to be vengeful, we would have rescued the girl intact. As it is, now there is nothing we can do. It seems to be an act of the gods," the driver stated calmly.

"Shut up. Act of the gods you say? You are all the same. Cruel, Insane!" Chelimo had detected a tinge of pride as the driver said 'act of the gods'.

"I am sorry but we have to wait for the break of day in order to get some rescue which will also take hours because it means bringing several excavators. Unfortunately, as you know madam, there is no other road which we can take," the IGP stated.

"Can't we walk?" Chelimo asked in desperation.

"In this hilly, slippery terrain madam? It would take us more than a day to walk the remaining distance to Kapchorwa. Madam, for now, we must surrender everything into God's hands because it is beyond our control," the uninvited driver was again commenting.

Chelimo did not want to listen to the man any more. He was pathetic, she decided. She went and slumped herself in the car, her body rocked by sobs.

"Maybe what my mother-in-law said is true: I just have bad luck," she cried in deep despair.

"My dear child, it is unfortunate that the secrets of the river have caught up with you as well. The fate of your mother, of your great-grandmothers awaits you. and what is tragic is that you don't even belong to the tribe," Chelimo said, her voice dripping with resignation and sadness.

The rain continued to gush out with a fury, the wind giving it momentum. The car too shook with the onslaught.

****

Because Daisy was a child born and raised in the city, away from the land of the Sabiny and ignorant of the ways of her mother's people, it was decided that it would not make sense to subject her to the normal pre-circumcision routine. She would be fast-tracked for reasons of expediency and privacy. It wasn't deemed prudent either, to present the much-sought after prize to police on a silver platter. There would be no dancing and her mother – for obvious reasons – would not be called to witness. A video camera manned by one of Adeni's men was the only witness. The Minister would want to enjoy a good view of the action, Adeni had assured his cohorts.

A combination of threats and a couple of violent swats across her face convinced Daisy that her only chance to survive and to see her mother again, lay in doing as she was told. So when she was asked to remove all her clothing, and put on the circumcision gear and walk with the *maturyondet* into the river, she said nothing.

She whimpered a little when she stepped into the cold river. She said nothing when the old woman's rough fingers found their way into her private parts and washed her.

Daisy still said nothing as she was helped out of the river, walked to what Adeni had christened 'the altar' and then asked to lay on her back carefully facing the morning sky. Adeni had ensured it was the same ground that her mother had been circumcised from. Daisy looked the perfect lamb for slaughter, as she lay helpless and resigned to her fate, tears flowing down her cheeks.

Her calm was disturbed by the old woman when she applied the pre-circumcision herbs onto her private parts. She jumped high and wild, screaming at the top of her tiny and tender voice, startling the women. Their concern though, was more of the need for strict privacy and secrecy, rather than anything to do with the girl's cowardice or lack of it - after all, she wasn't one of them. Had it been a normal circumcision event involving an actual daughter of Sebei; everybody would have taken issue with a candidate blinking, let alone screaming their heart out. But this was a different case.

The old women held her mouth as they soothingly assured her all would be well in just a little while. But the screams continued unabated as she felt a fire shoot through every part of her body and into her inner being. Years of sheltered life, protected like a gold fish in a sitting room aquarium had not prepared her for such eventualities. She was now a little fish that had been ejected from the aquarium right into the endless ocean, with neither preparation nor preamble.

Tears and mucus flowed down her face as she struggled with her captors, screaming as loud as she could, like a little duckling, in the grip of the wolf, and quacking for life, praying that her quacks would be heard by a kindred soul who'd come to her rescue before the wolf sank its canines into her rump. She now no longer cared what would or could happen to her; she simply screamed, even as the old women struggled to keep her quiet. They had not fully prepared for this eventuality; but the cameraman decided the scream-filled drama would make for great viewing for the Minister.

After what seemed like an eternity Daisy calmed down as her body became numb. She managed to stay still, but nobody wiped the tears and the mucus that remained on her face. Soon the tears caked, making her look like she had been - rather appropriately maybe - painted strips of white in honour of the ceremony.

"Child, you better steel up; we mean no harm at all," the surgeon was saying as she moved and picked one of the cruel looking, rusty curved knives that had been put on a rag as if for show. "You will ask any Sabiny woman and they will tell you this is the knife of redemption; the only thing that will make you a true ancestor of the Sabiny."

Daisy who had been having unexplained pains in her lower tummy moved uncomfortably. She was a pot-full of fear. She feared she was going to throw up. That she could have been poisoned. She had always heard that when people are poisoned they feel a lot of discomfort in the tummy. That's what everybody said when their neighbour died. But since she had refused to drink or eat anything they had offered her, she was almost sure that they had not poisoned her. She felt a wetness in her private parts and she feared that maybe she was wetting herself out of fear.

"Child, spread your legs further." Daisy did not spread her legs. "We do not have all the time, child. And don't you have any manners? Which child ignores instructions from an elder? You are stretching our patience."

She watched with horror as the old woman holding the knife edged forward toward her, wondering what exactly was going to happen to her.

Daisy tried to move but the old woman pinned her down with her knees. The other old women swung into action holding Daisy's arms down.

"It will be better for you to cooperate," the small-bodied woman said.

Daisy held her breath.

"Faster!" the woman holding the arms was saying.

"Please let me go. Let go of me!" Daisy shouted.

"Faster!" The woman holding Daisy's arms was urging the surgeon again.

"Leave me alone!" Daisy was shouting.

"Cut!"

"I can't!" the *mutik* said, her face creased in anger and disgust. Her hand, firmly holding *rotwet* had frozen midway to its target.

"Why?"

The *mutik* stood up abruptly and ordered, "release her!".

"Why?" several voices asked simultaneously, incredulously.

*****

The IGP and the Minister's team had waited a few hours behind the landslide after which the IGP called Kapchorwa police headquarters and asked for a vehicle to be sent to them. When the vehicle arrived, the Minister and the IGP got on board the green LandRover across the road.

Road-works commenced shortly after and in a short time, the road was clear. It did not take long before the drivers caught up with the green LandRover. Chelimo looked at the long line of vehicles following them and she sneered.

"What do we need all those vehicles for? To fetch my already mutilated baby? It doesn't matter anymore. Whether we get her today or after whatever length of time seems to be of no more consequence."

"Whatever the case, Madam, the earlier we find her, the better. She might need medication, for example. She might need food. She might need anything."

"Stop, stop!" Chelimo screamed.

"Well then?" the IGP said quietly. He was doing his best but he too was getting tired.

As he turned to move away, his phone rang. Chelimo jumped and almost grabbed the phone from him.

"Who is it?" the minister asked.

"It's the CID chief in charge of the search team in Kapchorwa," the IGP said.

"Any news?"

"I will find out in a minute," he said turning to speak on the phone.

"Any news?" The IGP asked.

"..."

"We might not be too late. Are you sure its only a few kilometres?"

"..."

"Thank you. According to the way you have described the area, it sounds like we are close by," the

IGP said as he beckoned Chelimo. "We shall be with you shortly," he said.

"..."

"Do not worry about the climbing and the slipperiness. We'll get there."

Chelimo could not wait any longer .

"What did they say?" she asked.

"We are close," the IGP said. "Please stay behind till we come for you."

The minister could not hear of that.

"Don't even think about it," she snapped.

"It might not be good for you."

"It's too late. I am already here with you." She moved on with them. Within a short time, the police had reached the location and surrounded it.

*****

"The girl is in the big hut sir," the CID chief said. Chelimo made a mad rush for the hut.

"Don't!" the CID tried to stop her but she was already gone. The IGP sprung into action and quickly held her to a stop. She turned and sunk all her teeth into his arm. He yanked off his arm and let go of her.

"She is my daughter not yours," Chelimo hissed at him.

"I am sorry madam but please let police accomplish its operation."

A few police officers dashed into the hut and within a minute they brought out Daisy.

"Mummy!!" she cried out as she ran towards her mother.

"Daisy!"

Chelimo stretched her arms and Daisy flew into them. Chelimo and her daughter wept in each other's arms. The men stared on, not knowing what to do.

"Was she alone?" The IGP asked.

"No sir. There were three other women. I believe they are the surgeonss. They are inside the hut, Sir."

"Arrest them!" one police officer shouted.

"But circumcision is not a crime," somebody else in the group cut in.

"No, it's not. Kidnapping is a crime though. It's a pity that these people genuinely believe that what they are doing is for the good of the tribe. Madam Minister, you have a long way to go with your people," the IGP said.

Chelimo was not listening to the IGP.

"Please tell me what they did to you," she was asking her daughter.

"They put herbs down there mummy and it hurt so bad! But maybe they wanted to sacrifice me because they had knives."

Everybody fell quiet to listen.

"And then?" Chelimo prompted her, impatiently, holding her breath.

"Then the old woman came down with a knife but shen she looked at me down there she said she could not cut..."

"You mean they did not c-c-cut you anywhere?"

"No mummy. They didn't cut me anywhere. "They forced my legs open. I tried to fight and kick but they held me firmly to the ground telling me not to waste my time and their time. The old woman held a curved knife and bent over between my legs, but suddenly she started cursing asking the other women why nobody told them that the girl was seeing the moon. They all exclaimed and said that it would be an abomination to cut me. They then released me from their grip."

Everybody clapped including the IGP.

"But how, my daughter? You have not started your periods yet."

"I did, while in that hut."

"But isn't she too young for that?" The IGP asked.

"Thirteen is not that early really. In any case it can happen when one is confronted with excessive stress, fear, tension, and anxiety. My daughter has been to hell and back."

"Why did you remain inside the hut?" Chelimo asked.

"Because one of the women said that they would keep me until their boss came and decided what my fate would be."

"Who is their boss? Who brought you here?"

"I don't know them mummy. They were all men."

At that point, two detectives emerged from the house, pushing three women.

"Don't," the IGP ordered. The detectives stood still. "These old women did not fetch the girl from Kampala. Leave them."

"Sir, don't we need them to assist us in investigations?"

"That, they will. But from their homes."

"That's okay sir."

Chelimo was shocked to see that she knew one of the women. The woman had lived under her roof for years as a housemaid. Memories of how the woman left Chelimo's home tumbled back.

Chelimo sighed. She knelt down and raised her eyes to the skies.

"Now I know that my redeemer lives!" she exclaimed, tears of joy streaming down her face.

Post- Script

The IGP and his team continued with investigations, looking for the kidnappers. Eventually, Adeni and his cronies were arrested and their whole plot right from the point at which they moved into the Minister's neighbourhood was exposed. The one that got away - quite predictably - was Arthur, who after the kidnap had found it necessary to try out the cereal in the cooler climes of Europe. He had no plans to return to Uganda especially because a software company had found his brilliant natural skills irresistible. He followed the Chelimo drama on his laptop, from the safety of a London flat.... over a bowl of cereal.

Chelimo finally found the nerve and guts to say 'yes' to another man. Mr. George Omondi, a civil engineering contractor and a single dad with one teenage son, had been one of many that had found the lovely Minister's "no" ironically a huge incentive to keep chasing her. Chelimo found him calm and quiet, compassionate and understanding; and blessed with a neat and original sense of humour. What tipped the scales when compared to other candidates was that Daisy instantly and immensely liked Mr. Omondi. Besides, Mr. Omondi's son who was two years older than Daisy had found in her the sister he never had. It was touch and go for the new little family; with each of the four members feeling that they had been issued a brand new lease of life and it couldn't begin soon enough. Dane learnt of the wedding as he watched the weekend news. Sarah, who was in the kitchen during the news bulletin and missed it completely, had slight trouble understanding why her husband (now a teetotaler) threw a stool at the television set before proceeding to kick it even after it had fallen and didn't look like it could fight back.

Chelimo remained the Minister for Culture and continued her crusade; mobilizing the many institutions that were fighting against Female Genital Mutilation. She was thrilled when in May 2011, the practice was outlawed in Uganda. He joy and pride knew no bounds when she addressed the nation in a live broadcast that was carried on all radio and television stations in the country.

"Today, we stand and hold up our heads for we have in place a law that will uphold the dignity of our women whose fate it has been to undergo the most cruel, the most inhuman practice, that of female genital mutilation. The government has given a blanket amnesty to all the surgeons who have been carrying out the operations because we know that they genuinely believed they were doing it for the good of women, and for the good of the tribe. But if any surgeon does not give herself in, then the law will take its course. The law is a very important milestone but on its own it is not enough. We must all get out and sensitize our people to shun this practice. And we must tell our people to embrace education because an educated parent cannot allow his or her daughter to go through that callous and calamitous practice.

"As you all know, my daughter Daisy Chemtai seated on my right [the cameras generously beamed on Daisy who beamed back, teeth flashing white] was kidnapped so she would be cut to spite me and those who have dared stand up against this evil practice. But God had a special plan to spare her and it is by His grace that the cruel knife returned home dry.

"I will tell you why she is called Chemtai. A dear childhood friend of mine called Chemtai who I was circumcised with did not make it beyond the knife. She died from her wounds shortly after we were cut. Many girls have died of circumcision-related complications but that is never talked about. Others are alive, but live a very difficult life, punctuated with unjust deprivation and undeserved suffering. Let's stand up strong against female circumcision. Let's adopt other respectful forms of passage into adulthood. Thank you for listening; may the Lord bless all those women out there who still bear a cross they were forced to carry and may the Lord bless Uganda," the Minister concluded.

Chelimo felt a sense of peace settle upon her. She was contented that such a day had come when she and all the women of her land had triumphed over the worst form of female oppression. It was upon the women to say no, since they now had the law on their side to protect them.

She knew however that the journey had just begun and she was under no illusion that it would be smooth all the way. Far from it.

She and other like-minded people and institutions would have to carry out massive campaigns to sensitise the women and girls and young men in Sebei as well as in other parts where cutting was being partised. Government would have to ensure that the law was enforced without fear or favour. Change would take time to settle in and take firm root; but it had begun and it was time to celebrate the new beginning.

Chelimo did not wipe the tears that flowed down her cheeks. She felt them cleanse her. She felt them cleanse her mother and her mother's mother. She felt them cleanse all the women who had been touched by the knife of wickedness called *rotwet*...

Printed in the United States
By Bookmasters